"Never speak to me like that again!"

Laura's words were a frosty command. "I'm your equal, Jared Eastern. I've just become your partner. And you're going to treat me that way. Because I won't accept anything else."

Before she could move away, he crushed her against him, his arms as unrelenting as hoops of steel. "I've had enough," he snarled. "You've tried my patience to the limit."

His chest heaved as he drew a breath and Laura didn't need to be psychic to sense that a turbulent violence within him was ready to explode. Fight or flight were out. To oppose him would be totally dangerous....

"Now kiss me!" he demanded fiercely. "Kiss me...because I'm going to kiss you. I'm going to kiss you until I find out what you really are."

EMMA DARCY nearly became an actress until her fiancé declared he preferred to attend the theater *with* her. She became a wife and mother. Later she took up oil painting—unsuccessfully, she remarks. Then, she tried architecture, designing the family home in New South Wales. Next came romance writing—"the hardest and most challenging of all the activities," she confesses.

Books by Emma Darcy

Don't miss any of our special offers. Write to us at the following address for information on our newest releases.

Harlequin Reader Service
P.O. Box 1397, Buffalo, NY 14240
Canadian address: P.O. Box 603,
Fort Erie, Ont. L2A 5X3

EMMA DARCY

bride of diamonds

Harlequin Books

TORONTO • NEW YORK • LONDON
AMSTERDAM • PARIS • SYDNEY • HAMBURG
STOCKHOLM • ATHENS • TOKYO • MILAN

Harlequin Presents first edition June 1991
ISBN 0-373-11367-6

Original hardcover edition published in 1990
by Mills & Boon Limited

BRIDE OF DIAMONDS

CHAPTER ONE

'WHY do you have to go back to Australia? What point is there?' Connie Hammond demanded in exasperation. 'I don't understand you, Laura.'

And that was the trouble, Laura thought. She and her mother would never reach an understanding. The rift between them had begun a long time ago and the only meeting-point left was the tie of blood. When all was said and done, they were still mother and daughter, and on that bond alone Laura tried to keep the peace.

'I want to go back, Mother,' she said quietly. 'It's as simple as that. And I did tell you when I came home for Christmas that I'd only be here for six weeks.'

Connie Hammond paced the bedroom carpet in agitation as her daughter continued packing her clothes into a well-worn and much-travelled suitcase.

She had never really aged, Laura thought. The dark, sculptured waves of her hair were carefully styled and lacquered in place. Her figure was fashionably slim and beautifully clothed. There was a mature look about her lovely face, but her skin looked untouched by the forty-six years of her life. No lines of worry. No stress. She was capable of leaving that behind her, even when she was upset, as she obviously was now. And while they were poles apart—and always would be—Laura could understand the drive that had taken her mother to the top of the social tree. The obsessional strain in her mother's nature was also in hers.

'It's this…this thing…you've got about your father, isn't it?' she said bitterly. 'What more do you have to know, for heaven's sake?'

Everything, Laura thought. She didn't say so. Up until a year ago she had known nothing of her real father. If the letter hadn't come, notifying her of the inheritance he had left her, she would still be ignorant of him. Only then had she been told the truth…under sufferance.

If it were at all possible, Connie Hammond would have wiped her first marriage from every record. She would have pretended that Andrew McKenzie had never existed at all, let alone fathered the child that had forced the wedding on her. Out of sight, out of mind, and she hated any reminder of her 'youthful mistake'. Thirty years ago, blue-blooded Bostonian girls did not have children out of wedlock. Not if they were to keep any shred of good reputation. Divorce, she found, was much more acceptable.

And after an acceptable period she had divorced Laura's father and married the kind of man she had always meant to marry. Ted Hammond was from an old Bostonian family, a respectable banker and a pillar of society. He had legally adopted Laura so that the McKenzie name need never be mentioned again. And it wouldn't have been…but for the letter. Only then had it all come out, and Laura had gone to Australia in search of the father she had never known.

The fact that her mother regarded Andrew McKenzie as a social misfit had aroused Laura's strongest sympathies. What she had learnt about his life intrigued her so much that she couldn't rest content until she knew why he had done what he'd done. She had to go back. That strange painting he had bequeathed to her held the key to the mystery—Laura was certain of it—and now that it was about to go on exhibition, someone somewhere might know what it meant.

She knew it was the slimmest of slim chances, and the decision she had made sat uneasily on her conscience. Her father had taken his secrets to the grave. Maybe she should let them rest there. But what she had done couldn't hurt him now. And she wanted to know! Needed to know! Had to know!

'What about Steven Hershaw?' her mother fired, moving on to another argument when she didn't get a response to work on.

'What about him?'

Connie Hammond heaved a defeated sigh at the uninterested tone. She sat down on the bed beside the suitcase in an attempt to force her wayward daughter's full attention.

'Laura, you're twenty-eight years old. Aren't you tired of wandering around the world? Of living in strange places?' She paused to emphasise her point. 'I know young women aren't supposed to rush into marriage these days, but men don't wait around forever to choose their wives. Steven Hershaw is one of the most eligible bachelors in Boston. He's interested in you . . .'

'He thinks I'd be an ornament to his life,' Laura commented. She lifted eyes that were full of gentle mockery. 'He wouldn't have thought that a few years ago, would he?'

Connie Hammond winced. 'Everyone's forgotten about that, Laura.'

But Laura hadn't. She never would. Her perception of so many things had been changed by all those adolescent years when the tortured chemistry of her puberty had erupted on her skin and blighted her life with its ugliness. No one had wanted to be her friend then. She knew all about being a social misfit. An outcast.

The cruelties perpetrated on Laura Hammond by her so-called peers had been subtle and many, enough to make her withdraw into herself so deeply that Connie

Hammond had taken her daughter to a psychiatrist for remedial treatment. But the cure had had nothing to do with any sickness of the mind. The cure had come with the new laser technology treatment which had burnt away the cells that had caused her disfigurement and turned her into a social embarrassment.

Her skin was now as fine and smooth as a child's. Without blemish. Her gangly, graceless figure had filled out to accommodate her bone-structure in a way that was strikingly feminine. She had learnt to stand tall, with her shoulders squared and her chin high, and the grey eyes returned anyone's gaze with a serene and confident directness, no longer inclined to flinch from anyone or anything. She was socially acceptable now. Eminently desirable. An ornament that would grace any man's life.

The purely drawn features of her face were perfectly balanced, although Connie Hammond would have preferred a more vivacious expression to the quiet beauty which sometimes seemed like a mask, shutting people out. Privately she wished Laura would make something more of her thick black hair which she wore long and straight and clipped back at the nape of her neck. The severe style suited her well enough, but it was not at all fashionable. To Connie Hammond, fashion counted in this world. But she knew if she said anything about it— anything at all about Laura's appearance—the grey eyes would fill with the gentle mockery she hated.

'What are you looking for, Laura?' she asked tiredly. 'What do you want?'

The long, nimble fingers paused in the act of folding a blouse. A whimsical smile curved her mouth. 'Perhaps I'm searching for what life is all about. Who knows? What I do know is that I don't want Steven Hershaw, nor the kind of life he'd want me to lead.'

'It's a good life, Laura,' Connie argued on a note of desperation. She had done her utmost to promote the match, hoping that Laura would finally take her place where she belonged. This was her home. Why couldn't she be happy here?

To Connie Hammond, Boston and its exclusive set of people was the only world worth knowing. Nothing could be better. To Laura, if something else wasn't better, then life wasn't worth living at all. She had grimly survived her miserable adolescence by telling herself that this narrow-minded society—where appearances counted far more than the person inside—was only a drop in the ocean of humanity.

As soon as she was through college, she had gone into the travel business. With the concessions and discounts available to her, and living on a shoestring budget, she had worked her way around most of the world. There were so many different ways of life; different customs, different values, different priorities—some better, some worse. And Boston was certainly not at the bottom of the scale. Far from it. But to Laura it could only ever be a prison she had to escape from. The alienation had gone too deep for her to ever fit comfortably and contentedly into the life her mother led.

She looked up, and her heart twisted at the sad disappointment in her mother's eyes. 'I'm sorry,' she said softly. 'I truly am sorry I can't be the daughter you want me to be. But what's right for you is not right for me, and I have to go my own way, Mother.'

Connie Hammond shook her head. 'I've tried so hard...and you can't say Ted hasn't been a good father... We've done everything we could for you...'

'Please don't think I'm not grateful,' Laura put in quickly, pained by her mother's pain. 'I love you both and I don't want you to be hurt. It's just that...' She lifted her hands helplessly. Impossible to explain without hurting. She fought against feeling guilty, determined not to give in to emotional blackmail. 'Mother, you made your choices,' she said flatly. 'Let me make mine.'

A brooding disapproval settled on her mother's brow. 'He gave you up without a backward glance,' she shot out bitterly.

Laura could well imagine how Andrew McKenzie would have been frozen out of the marriage, left without a leg to stand on as far as custody of a baby was concerned. Her father might have thought Laura was better off without him in her life. Undoubtedly Connie Hammond would have projected that. But Andrew McKenzie hadn't forgotten his daughter. And Laura couldn't explain to her mother the strange affinity she now felt with him, even though he was dead and buried.

She made another effort to keep the peace. 'Mother, I'm not turning my back on you. I'll keep in touch, just as I've always done. I'm sorry if that's not enough for you, but I have to lead my own life as I see fit. Can't we leave it at that?'

As much as she privately railed against it, Connie Hammond recognised defeat. The closed look on Laura's face warned her she was pushing too far, and she had to keep the door open for her return. One day she might finally see what was best for her. After all, Laura was more her daughter than Andrew McKenzie's.

But Connie Hammond didn't know, and she never would know, the sense of freedom that lifted Laura's soul as she flew out of Boston the next morning, en route to a country on the other side of the earth—the land 'down under'. Nor would she have been in any sympathy with the mixed feelings that coursed through Laura five nights later as she stood in the New South Wales Art Gallery, staring up at the Andy Mac painting that was so different from all the others.

The yearning to understand mixed uncomfortably with a persistent sense of guilt. From the first moment Laura had seen it, she had sensed that the painting held an intensely private meaning, so full of poignant feeling that it had tugged at her heart in some indefinable way. She shouldn't have put it on public exhibition, yet the compulsion to know what it meant had overridden every other consideration. If enough people saw it...if someone could tell her... Was it so wrong to want to find out about her father?

It was a strange picture, savage but fascinating. The sun was setting behind a red limestone range, throwing a coral-rose stain across the sky. In the foreground was a straw-pale plain, swathed with a misty blue from which struggled the gnarled limbs of giant baobab trees. In the top left-hand corner was a woman's face, weirdly integrated with the patterned sky, part of it, yet apart, and somehow projecting a timeless ache that could never be appeased.

Her father had not given the painting a name. It was not even signed. He had told Jeremy Bursell that it was never to be sold, not in any circumstances. And, although the artist's hand was undoubtedly her father's, this painting was totally uncharacteristic of all his other work, not only in mood, but in subject.

Laura sensed it was the key to the lost years, the key to the mystery of why Andrew McKenzie, geologist, had become Andy Mac, the artist—a reclusive, eccentric loner who had spent the last twenty years of his life in Port Douglas on the far north coast of Queensland. In all that time he had never spoken to anyone about his past. No one in Port Douglas had even known he had a daughter until Laura had turned up to claim her inheritance. It surprised them. Andy Mac had particularly shied clear of women.

What had happened in those years between the end of his brief marriage to her mother and his arrival in Port Douglas? Why had he changed his life so radically?

And why had he never got in touch with her? He must have thought of her—the daughter he had given up—or he wouldn't have left her his house and the paintings.

'*Lost Dreams,*' someone said behind her, obviously reading from the catalogue. It was the name Laura had given the painting for the exhibition.

'Unusual, isn't it?' a woman's voice commented.

'Fascinating.'

Laura knew, with absolute certainty, how unusual and fascinating it was. The scene depicted was somewhere in the Kimberley, a remote corner of Western Australia which was one of the last frontiers settled by civilised man, the land the old bushmen had called 'west-o'-sunset', and which—geologically—was one of the oldest land regions in the world. She had even identified the limestone range in the background as the King Leopold Range. Unfortunately she had found no other answers on her trip there. Not even professional safari agents would take her off the few tourist tracks that were considered safe.

'This is the Top End, lady,' she was told. 'There's no one close you can holler to for help. If you get lost, that's it!'

The inhabitants were few and far between. They were mainly located on cattle stations, the smallest of which were at least a few hundred square miles in area. She had seen the sunset over the King Leopold Range and it had been as fantastic as it had been painted in *Lost Dreams*. She had seen straw-pale plains and baobab trees. She had seen the ancient sandstone plateau of the Bungle Bungles with its huge outcrop of beehive rocks, and the Stanley Chasms where the canyons were so narrow that they never saw sunlight. It was a strange primeval land which she could well believe was one of the oldest regions in the world. But no one she had talked to could

remember an Andrew McKenzie. And she hadn't seen
the place he had painted.

What had happened there?

Why had he painted the woman's face into the scene?

And whose was the face...so beautiful...haunting?

Laura heaved a sigh of frustration and turned away.
She knew it was the thinnest of thin hopes that showing
Lost Dreams would bring the answers that she wanted.
Yet what else could she do? With all her other enquiries
about her father she had come to a dead end.

The request that a selection of her father's work be
shown in a special collection of Australian art had given
her the idea. The collection would be shown in every
State capital. This was the first night—the opening night
of the exhibition in Sydney—and, from the size of the
crowd that had attended, Laura figured that a great many
people would eventually see the painting. Perhaps it
would stir some helpful comment.

Her gaze wandered idly around the people milling
through the gallery. And then she saw him. He was in
the adjoining room but coming towards her—the most
striking man Laura had ever seen in her life. Not a pretty-
boy, not classically handsome, he had a presence that
emanated command.

He was tall and his three-piece fawn suit graced a
powerful physique. His skin was deeply tanned, his hair
sun-kissed—blonde and caramel, straight and slightly
shaggy. He had a strong, arresting face, brow, cheek-
bones and jawline...all firm, uncluttered, barely fleshed.
No line of weakness anywhere.

It was a hard face, carved with determined purpose
and set for a destiny of his own making. The weather-
beaten skin had seen too much sun and it was stretched
tightly over the strong bones. The eyes were too deeply
socketed for Laura to see their colour; his nose was
almost hawkish; his lips sharply defined, full enough to

hint at sensuality, but there was a controlled set to his mouth that denied any self-indulgence.

He was a world away from Steven Hershaw in more ways than simply distance, Laura thought, feeling a tug of attraction that was disturbingly primitive. She could imagine this man leading a wagon-train into Indian territory, or commanding a Roman Legion, or riding beside Genghis Khan. He would make his own rules, and heaven help anyone who opposed him.

She brushed the fanciful thoughts away. 'What do you want?' her mother had asked, and Laura wondered if she would ever want a man who looked like him. It would certainly be interesting to find out, she thought, and smiled at her wild imaginings.

Whether he sensed her speculative scrutiny or whether her smile had caught his eye Laura did not know, but as he reached the archway into the room he paused in his step and looked straight at her. Laura had been looked at by a lot of men since her face had been cleared of all disfigurement, but never with such devastating directness.

Usually she dismissed such attention with cynical amusement. But this was more than a fleeting appraisal of desirability, more than an appreciation of her flawless face and the curvaceous femininity of her figure. It was a self-possessed assessment which somehow projected the confident knowledge that he could have her if he wanted to. The only question was whether it was worth the effort.

Despite the elegant clothes she had worn for this formal opening night—the white organza blouse with its black-edged frills, the slim black silk skirt that was fashionably slit up the back seam—Laura felt like a naked slave girl standing on an auction block, waiting for the hammer to fall. Her whole body was tense. Her heart was in her mouth. When someone touched her arm she almost jumped.

'Sorry if I startled you.'

It was Jeremy Bursell, the dealer in fine arts who had 'discovered' Andy Mac some years ago. He had handled all her father's business since then. He smiled at her, a rotund, affable, but very shrewd businessman in his late forties, who was only too pleased to be dealing with a client whose inheritance would bring him huge commissions.

'Are you satisfied with the hanging of your father's paintings?' he asked. 'I supervised the lighting myself.'

'Fine. Really fine. I'm sure my father would be pleased if he could see them right now. They look good, don't they?' she answered quickly.

'They are good,' he said with the confidence of a man who knew the art world inside out. 'I'm relieved you're not in a rush to sell. The price on your father's work will keep going up in leaps and bounds now that he's...er...dead. I expect this exhibition to arouse even more interest, and the longer we hold off...'

Laura darted a glance back at the archway, but the man had turned his attention away from her. He still stood in the same place, as immobile as if turned to stone, the muscles of his face tightened and concentrated. Then the weight of his body moved imperatively forward, like a boxer preparing to strike, or more like a bolt of lightning making ready to blaze forth. His air of explosive tension was so pronounced that Laura followed the direction of his fixed gaze, oddly piqued that his interest in her had been so totally diverted.

A *frisson* of shock ran through her heart as she realised he was staring at *Lost Dreams*. In the next instant he propelled himself forward, a few lithe strides bringing him face to face with the painting. He shook his head as if in disbelief, then after several moments he opened

the catalogue he carried and leafed through it, obviously
looking for the listings.

He read what there was to read, then studied the
painting again. The catalogue slowly crumpled in the
hand that tightened into a closed fist. He swung around,
his face set in determined purpose, his eyes scanning
quickly over the people in the room. They passed over
Laura without a flicker of recognition...green
eyes...glittering with a savagery that more than suggested he would not tolerate anyone or anything getting
in his way.

He was off and moving swiftly through the adjoining
room before Laura recollected herself enough to wonder
what fascination had attracted him to the painting. Why
had he reacted to it so strongly? Had the strangely
primitive scene called to something in his soul? Yet he
seemed to have dismissed it as abruptly and totally as
he had dismissed any interest in her.

She suddenly felt very tired. Jet lag still catching up
on her, she thought, and excused herself from Jeremy
Bursell's self-serving conversation. It was not a long walk
back from the gallery to her hotel, and the exercise helped
her shake off the disturbing incident with the man.

It was probably pointless to hang around the gallery
anyway, fantasising possibilities from people's reactions
to *Lost Dreams*. She had to do something more positive.

The doorman at the Sheraton-Wentworth smiled a
welcome greeting as she entered the foyer. The hotel was
centrally located in the city and all the staff were friendly.
'If you must go travelling, always stay at a Sheraton,'
her mother had advised. 'It's safe.'

Laura glanced up at the glittering chandeliers and
smiled to herself as she remembered the cheap hostels
and lodgings she had stayed in over the years. She had
the money to treat herself to comfort now. The last Andy
Mac painting sold had fetched over fifty thousand

dollars, and if Jeremy Bursell was right about the increasing demand for her father's work she might never have to work again for the rest of her life.

An idea came to her as she prepared for bed. She wasn't used to having a great deal of money at her disposal, and she hadn't thought of it the last time she went to the Kimberley, but she could now afford to hire a helicopter to fly over the whole area. She still had the photographs she had taken of the painting. If she spotted any likely place, the helicopter could land there. What she would achieve by it she wasn't sure, but the compulsion to keep on looking for answers could not be denied.

Despite the fatigue that seemed to have seeped into every bone in her body, Laura was still awake when the telephone rang an hour later. She glanced at the digital clock set in the bedside table, mentally adding nine hours to the time. In Boston, her parents would have just finished breakfast. Laura propped herself up on the pillows and lifted the telephone receiver, resigned to assuring her mother that she was safe and sound and would write soon.

But it wasn't an international call.

'Sorry if I've disturbed you, Laura,' Jeremy Bursell rattled out over the line, 'but there's been an offer made for one of your father's paintings and I've been pressed to close the deal as soon as possible. If you're agreeable.'

An odd feeling of premonition crawled down Laura's spine. Why call her tonight? What was the urgency? 'Which painting is the buyer interested in?' she asked. But she knew what the answer would be even before he replied.

Jeremy cleared his throat as if the issue stuck in his craw. *'Lost Dreams.'*

Her heart gave an agitated skip. She had been right!

Jeremy rushed on, obviously anxious to defer the response he knew would come from her. 'The client has been informed, as per your instructions, that *Lost Dreams* is not for sale. However, the offer he is making...money is no object, Laura. I did not feel I could take it upon myself to refuse without consulting you.'

'You know I can't sell it. You told me yourself what my father said,' she reminded him.

'I know...I know,' he repeated in barely held exasperation. 'But, Laura, it wasn't written into his will. There's no legality binding you. I'm sure he wouldn't hold you to that trust if he knew...' He took a deep breath. 'Laura, this is big...'

'Not big enough, Jeremy.' Never to be sold, her father had said. He would rather the painting be destroyed than sold—although he had never destroyed it himself. It had held some deeply personal significance for him, something...

'You don't think five million dollars is big enough?'

Stunned disbelief brought Laura's thoughts to a screaming halt. She shook her head, unable to accept that she had heard correctly. 'I'm going deaf, Jeremy. Would you please repeat that?'

'Five...million...dollars!'

It took a few more stunned moments before she managed to speak again. 'I don't believe this is happening.'

'Neither do I,' Jeremy replied with feeling, but she sensed the eager excitement he was suppressing. The commission on five million dollars was obviously dangling before his eyes.

Laura's mind finally moved into full gear. Someone wanted that painting very badly. The question was...why? And Laura wanted that knowledge very badly.

'Who is the buyer?' she asked.

'I don't know. In this type of situation, the bids always come through a third party. People don't wish to focus themselves in the spotlight. However, I can assure you the bid is completely bona fide.'

Laura took a deep breath. She had to figure this out carefully. Make the right decisions to get what she wanted. Excitement rippled through her. This was what she had been hoping for—the reason the painting had been put on exhibition—and the response was breathtaking! And she could blow it if she wasn't careful! She suppressed the excitement. When she spoke it was in a cool, detached voice.

'Jeremy, tell the intermediaries that on this painting I will only deal with the principals. In person. No agents.'

'Just a moment. I'll get them on the other phone.'

She waited, her tension growing as the minutes ticked by. Ten minutes. Fifteen minutes. All the exhilaration drained away with the waiting. She felt desperately tired, but her mind kept working at fever pitch. Apparently her demand was meeting with resistance. A great deal of resistance. Who was it who didn't want to be known? How many people in Australia had that kind of money to throw away on a painting? Was there a list of millionaires that she could look up and assess for some connection to her father?

At last Jeremy came back on the line.

'Laura, the principal is quite adamant that he only wishes to purchase the painting. He is not prepared to discuss the matter at all. I'm led to believe that is the reason he made the purchase offer such an extraordinary amount of money. It's a take-it-or-leave-it situation. Walk in, walk out. You've got to decide. If you walk away from this you'll never get him back.'

Laura took her time considering the position. This was like playing poker. But she had never played for stakes as high as this before. The principle was clear: if she didn't find out who the buyer was, she would probably never find out about her father. And if someone was prepared to offer that much, she didn't believe it was a 'leave it' situation. The position might be 'take it', but it was almost certainly not 'leave it'. This had to be a bluff to get a quick decision from her.

In any case, nothing could persuade her to give up that painting. Not when she had turned the corner and was heading up the straight to the finishing line. She knew now, without a doubt, that *Lost Dreams* held some special significance to someone else besides her father. She breathed in deeply, needing to slow her adrenalin and pulse-rate before throwing down the gauntlet.

'No,' she said flatly. 'The answer is *no*, Jeremy. Definitely no sale under these conditions. But if he changes his mind—I'm presuming the interested party is a man— I'll discuss the business with him. He can ring me here or leave a message. But until he is prepared to give me what I want, the answer is *no*!'

'Laura...' She could hear the hiss of his breath as Jeremy bit back a protest. 'As you wish. Do you want to hold on while I pass on your reply?'

'I'm tired, Jeremy. Ring me back.'

'Tired...' Obviously Jeremy was so pumped up himself he couldn't believe her response. He manfully swallowed down any comment. 'As you wish,' he repeated, and hung up.

Laura slid back down on the pillows and tried to relax. It was utterly impossible. Her mind kept racing backwards and forwards. Had she played the right hand? She couldn't really plan her next move until the buyer made his response, but that didn't stop her considering the possibilities.

It was a longer wait this time, but Laura didn't mind. Each minute that passed increased her hope that a personal meeting might be effected. Obviously a lot of people were talking very seriously, and she had no doubt that Jeremy was doing his best to keep the deal alive.

The telephone rang. She snatched up the receiver.

'Laura...' The note of relief in Jeremy's voice brought an exultant smile to Laura's lips. 'Assurances are wanted. The principal insists that the meeting be completely confidential.'

'Absolutely,' she agreed quickly.

'And it has to be tomorrow morning. As early as you can make it.'

Laura needed as much time with him as possible. The man was totally impatient and would almost certainly be reluctant to discuss anything. And since she was in the box-seat at the moment, she could make her own terms.

'Invite him to join me for breakfast at my hotel. The Garden Court Restaurant. Eight-thirty.'

There was only a short pause before Jeremy came back with the reply. 'Agreed.'

'Fine! What's his name, Jeremy?'

'Not given. I had to supply yours. Will you sell, Laura?'

Caution held her tongue. She didn't want any argument over the deal. 'I'll listen. Thank you for negotiating the meeting, Jeremy. I'll let you know what comes of it. Whatever way it goes, you'll be recompensed for your trouble.'

'I'd better be there tomorrow too, Laura,' he said quickly.

'No, Jeremy. I'm sorry. Any other deal but not this one. This is totally private.'

He heaved a reluctant sigh. 'OK. Good luck.'

'Thank you. For everything. Goodnight, Jeremy.'

She hung up quickly, but excitement kept sleep at bay for so long that she ended up ordering a wake-up call for the morning, anxious to be well and truly prepared for what was coming.

It could very well be a long-shot that the man had known her father, that the painting meant something personal to him, but five million dollars spelled out a compulsive desire to acquire, and there had to be a reason for it over and above the usual appreciation of an art-lover. It could hardly be an investment buy at that price. So that left . . . what?

CHAPTER TWO

LAURA left her room at eight-fifteen and took the lift down to the fifth floor. From this level, the higher section of the hotel curved around a roof-garden—ornamental trees in huge tubs and well-clipped hedges that provided a pleasant view through the glass wall of the main restaurant. One could even see to the Domain Park where the New South Wales Art Gallery was situated.

Laura gave her name to the waiter who greeted her, informed him that she was expecting a business acquaintance to join her, and requested a table near the glass entrance doors to the Garden Court Restaurant. She wanted to watch the arrivals from the lift, to assess the prospective buyer before he identified her. If he knew anything meaningful about that painting he should be approximately in the same age-group as her parents.

She had dressed accordingly. Her long thick hair was twisted up into a tidy topknot. She wore a pink linen suit with a crisp white blouse. She hoped the man would not be too difficult to handle. Australians were not the same as Americans. She had found them to be disconcertingly direct at times, and this man obviously didn't want his time wasted. She would certainly need all her wits about her to pace the conversation and lead towards what she wanted to know.

The waiter obligingly ushered her to the nearest table for two. She took the chair which gave her an unobstructed view of the foyer. Coffee was immediately offered and she accepted it gratefully. During the next ten minutes only couples emerged from the lift.

23

Laura could hardly believe her eyes when she saw him again—the man who had made such a strong and disturbing impact on her at the gallery last night—but there was no mistaking him. He was even wearing the same three-piece fawn suit.

She stared at him, her pulse fluttering in agitation as she wondered... But he couldn't be the man she had to meet. He looked to be in his mid-thirties, not old enough to be of any use to her. Not in the way that she needed. Not old enough to be a man who had known her father and what had happened with his life over twenty years ago. This man would only have been a boy then.

He checked his watch as he entered the restaurant then caught her stare as he lifted his head. She saw the flash of recognition. His mouth twisted with cynical amusement. There could be no doubt he remembered last night's brief encounter and Laura was mortified at being caught showing interest in him a second time. She jerked her head away and stared out at the roof-garden, hoping he would be seated at the other end of the room. The last thing she needed this morning was to be distracted by him.

She took a deep breath to calm her nerves, counted slowly to twenty, then checked her own watch. It was right on the dot of eight-thirty.

'Miss Hammond?'

She gritted her teeth. It was him. Had to be. There hadn't been time for anyone else to enter, enquire about her, and approach her table. And the voice fitted... a low, honey-textured tone with a hard edge. Laura wasn't given to blushing, but embarrassment sent a surge of warmth up her long throat and she could feel heat suffusing over her cheeks. If he thought she was an easy pick-up, she had to disabuse him of the notion fast. Mighty fast. Otherwise she might be compromised as far as the all-important meeting was concerned.

Her face might have reddened, but the imperative need to keep this man at arm's length, to get rid of him, quickly made her eyes as impersonal and remote as the King Leopold Range. However, when she turned her gaze up to his, he gave no indication that he received the message.

'May I join you?' he asked politely, and there was not the slightest spark of amusement or any hint of flirtatious invitation in the green eyes that bored into hers. They were hard. Hard and purposeful.

'I'm sorry,' she said with as much cool composure as she could manage. Despite the urgency she felt, she experienced a twinge of disappointment. In other circumstances . . . but not now. 'Some other time, perhaps. I'm expecting—'

'Me. You're expecting me, Miss Hammond. We have a purchase to discuss. If you wish to.'

'You?' It slipped out before Laura could bite it back. And it was a mistake. She sensed the satisfaction that brought a thin smile to his hawkish warrior's face.

'My name is Jared Eastern,' he said, and offered his hand. His eyes sharpened on hers as he added, 'If that means anything to you.'

His skin was taut and tough, as if he had done a great deal of hard manual labour. Even his light grasp gave Laura a quivery feeling of feminine weakness and she quickly withdrew her hand.

'I'm afraid not,' she replied. 'I don't move in financial circles. And, of course, I'm not an Australian.'

'Ah!'

And again came the strong sense that her answer had given him satisfaction. This was wrong, Laura thought. He was learning too much about her, and she was here to pump him for information. The poise she needed for this meeting was badly shaken and it took an act of considerable will-power to recover some of it. She nodded towards the opposite chair.

'Please sit down, Mr Eastern. I beg your pardon for my lack of greeting. I must confess I was anticipating someone much older.'

'So was I. But I don't mind being pleasantly surprised.' It was said with a charming smile that didn't quite reach his eyes. He sat down and regarded her with speculative interest. 'Your accent tells me you're an American. Is that the problem with my offer?'

'I have no problem being an American, Mr Eastern,' she replied, deliberately misunderstanding him in order to play for time. 'Shall we order now?' she added, and smiled an invitation at the hovering waiter without waiting for an answer.

The waiter obliged by handing them menus. Jared Eastern flicked Laura a derisive look before lowering his gaze to the breakfast listings. He waited until the orders were taken, more coffee was poured, and the waiter had withdrawn.

'I was enquiring if the currency was a problem,' he resumed. 'I appreciate that international money exchange can create difficulties. I assure you we can work around that.'

'Oh? And who is we?' Laura asked. She burned with the memory of the way he had looked at her last night, and this morning's mistake only added fuel to the fire. 'Who are you?'

Something dangerous flickered in his eyes. 'You and I, Miss Hammond, are *we*. Aren't we here to discuss ways and means? As for myself, my financial rating is——'

'First-rate,' she supplied drily.

'Thank you.'

He was not going to give anything away. But she was beginning to relish the challenge he posed. He was not going to find her an easy doormat to walk all over. She smiled. 'I would like to know what facilities you have for working around international currency problems.'

The dangerous gleam receded. 'A company with worldwide connections. We have an office in New York. What part of the USA are you from?'

'Boston. Massachusetts. Not so far from New York. Not as far as Sydney.'

'I'm acquainted with Boston, Miss Hammond,' he said drily. 'Now, shall we get down to business?'

'Would you mind telling me first what business you are in, Mr Eastern?'

'I dig things out of the ground,' he said with sardonic amusement.

'That must be profitable for you. But what kind of things?'

His eyes mocked her interest. 'The kind of things that the very most beautiful women, like yourself, consider their very best friends. Diamonds, Miss Hammond. The finest coloured diamonds in the world.'

The Bendeneer diamond-mine in the Kimberley! She had read about it. But it had been established in the seventies, long after her father had arrived at Port Douglas. She had dismissed any connection to it when she had last visited the area. The timing seemed wrong. But maybe she was mistaken about that. Her father had been a geologist. How long did it take to establish a mine after diamond deposits had been found? But why would her father leave if he'd found diamonds?

'You wanted to discuss my proposal. Let's discuss it,' Jared Eastern pushed. 'You start first. Ladies before gentlemen. What precisely do you want, Miss Hammond?'

Laura hesitated. If she told him precisely what she wanted—the reason behind his need to buy the painting...and need it had to be, for the extraordinary amount of money he was prepared to pay—he could easily tell her the first lot of nonsense that came into his head. Finesse was required. Stealth and treachery, if necessary. As far as this matter was concerned. she would be just as ruthless as he was at getting his own way, she thought grimly.

Even if he had nothing to tell her about her father, she wanted her curiosity satisfied about Jared Eastern's motives. She had not forgotten his strong reaction to the painting last night. It had completely blotted out his interest in her. Not that she wanted his interest, but...he certainly had some explaining to do.

She hadn't liked the cynical remark he had made, including her among the beautiful women who valued diamonds above all else. At the moment, though, it was better not to tell him she was one woman who could not be bought. Not for five million or even five billion dollars. He would find that out soon enough.

'To tell you the truth, Mr Eastern, I'm not sure I want to sell you *Lost Dreams*,' she said flatly. 'Why do you want to buy it?'

The waiter returned to serve them glasses of freshly squeezed orange juice. Jared Eastern downed his immediately, then raised a flint-hard gaze. 'I'm making a name for myself in art circles. A collector of unique works,' he replied sardonically. 'I'll make this the 'Purchase of The Year'. I'll accommodate your taxation problems as far as I can, Miss Hammond, but that's as far as I go. The offer is as it stands. And after today, it won't stand.'

She held his gaze, trying to probe behind the words. 'You misunderstand me, Mr Eastern,' she retorted evenly. 'It's not a question of money. That will not influence my decision—when I make it. It's a question of why you want that particular painting. Unless you tell me that, I can assure you that you have no chance of acquiring *Lost Dreams*. Take it or leave it. And after today, that offer won't stand either.'

His head jerked back almost imperceptibly. But Laura saw it. She knew she had just played a wild card, made a throw into the playing ring that Jared Eastern had not calculated on. And she had surprised him.

She lifted her glass and sipped the juice as he weighed her words. She was thankful her hands were steady. Her heart was pumping overtime and there was a zing in her blood that she had never felt before.

His mouth took on a sardonic twist. 'Curiosity killed the cat, Miss Hammond. You have five million reasons for not murdering this deal. What induces you to put a question mark on it?'

'Until you give me five million reasons to answer that question, Mr Eastern, I'm afraid the information is confidential.'

He considered her for several moments before he spoke again, but he gave no sign of any disturbance of mind this time. Nevertheless, Laura could almost hear the calculations ticking fast and furiously behind those guarded green eyes.

'It would seem we have reached an impasse. But we have a day to sort it out,' he said lightly. 'And since it may very well take the whole day—at the rate we're going—I would ask, as a sign of good faith from you, that the painting be withdrawn from the exhibition for the next twenty-four hours.'

The request struck Laura as unusual. As curious, in fact, as all the other facets of this deal. First the incredible offer that had forced Jeremy's hand last night. Then the insistence on meeting with her as early as possible this morning. Now, when more delay was being incurred, Jared Eastern wanted the painting out of the gallery.

The answer shot into Laura's mind. He didn't want it to be seen! He couldn't stand to have it on public exhibition. That was what this was all about. It wasn't so much a need to acquire, but a need to get it out of circulation!

'I'm sorry, Mr Eastern, but I won't do that unless you tell me why you want it withdrawn.'

'I gave you a reason,' he reminded her with a slight touch of impatience.

'I'm afraid it's not good enough,' Laura insisted.

He shook his head in a bemused fashion. 'I give you reasons. You won't accept them. How can I prove them to you?' He gave her a smile that appealed for her indulgence. 'Perhaps we got off on the wrong foot to start with. Did I offend you at the gallery last night?'

The unexpected switch to a more personal basis threw Laura into confusion for a moment. 'Offend me? How could you do that?' she answered weakly.

'No? Then I shall do what I was tempted to do when I first saw you. The timing now is not so good but it will have to suffice. You appear somewhat high-strung. Champagne with breakfast might loosen you up.'

He signalled the waiter and asked for a bottle of Bollinger, cost no object. When he turned back to Laura, the green eyes danced with a host of suggestive possibilities. And what looked like a strong dash of unholy mirth. 'Do you have champagne for breakfast frequently, Miss Hammond?'

He was patronising her!

Undoubtedly he was used to women staring at him, and with his combination of looks and wealth he was used to getting any woman he wanted. But if he thought she could be won over by a bit of gratuitous charm, he was way out in left field. And when it came to patronising, she'd been through one of the best training grounds in the world.

'Champagne breakfasts are one of my mother's specialities,' she said matter-of-factly, and as a little exercise in one-up-manship she added, 'The Hammonds are a long-established banking family in Boston, Mr Eastern.'

It didn't put him down at all. His eyes sparkled a mocking reproach. 'You told me you didn't move in financial circles. Shame on you, Miss Hammond.'

She shrugged. 'I'm not interested in banking.'

'No. Naturally not,' he drawled. 'I imagine the arts are more your style.'

She gave him a Mona Lisa smile, not affirming or contradicting. Let him wonder if he'd made a mistake!

He regarded her with a musing expression for several moments before trying a new tack. 'You are quite tantalisingly beautiful. But I dare say you've been told that many times.'

The flattery was like water off a duck's back to Laura. 'You have quite an interesting face yourself, Mr Eastern. I thought so last night. But I'm sure you're aware of that. What I find even more interesting is the face in the painting.'

His eyes narrowed, but not before she saw a flash of some intense emotion. Anger? Resentment? 'Yes. Quite intriguing the way it's been integrated with the background. An artistic *tour-de-force*. I've never seen anything like it,' he said smoothly. 'That's one of the reasons I want to buy it,' he added pointedly.

Laura was quite certain that he spoke the truth on that score, but still he wasn't giving anything away.

The champagne arrived and was poured into glasses. Jared Eastern lifted his in a toast. 'To a better understanding between us,' he said with a smile that raised a slight flutter in her heart.

He was almost compellingly attractive. Laura struggled to fend off his strongly masculine sex appeal. She could not afford to let him get to her. Besides, who knew better than she that the person inside was more important than an attractive exterior?

Determined to keep her mind clear, she took only the smallest sip of champagne and was grateful when their breakfast order was served immediately afterwards.

She reviewed the situation as she began on her Eggs Benedict. Jared Eastern was not going to be trapped into saying anything he didn't want to say. He was too sharp, too clever, and far too manipulative to allow himself to be led beyond where he wanted to go.

But she had learnt something.

He wanted the painting out of the exhibition.

It couldn't be the scene of the Kimberley that concerned him so much. It had to be the woman's face. And that meant it was recognisable. Not only recognisable, but it was of some very real and urgent significance to him that it not be recognised by anyone else. Now that she knew who *he* was, Laura figured she could find out who the woman was. But would she be any more forthcoming than Jared Eastern?

'How long have you owned the painting?'

She glanced up sharply, but there was only a mildly quizzical look on his face. 'Since last year.'

'I noticed in the catalogue that the artist died last year. Did you acquire the painting before or after his death?'

'After,' Laura answered briefly. Was it time now to reveal that the artist was her father? She wasn't sure if that information would draw more openness from Jared Eastern, or close him up even tighter.

'Then you haven't had it very long,' he commented, and again Laura sensed his satisfaction in her reply. The artist was dead, and his secrets buried with him. That was what Jared Eastern thought. If she jolted him now with her relationship to Andy Mac, it might jolt him out of his self-satisfaction, but it wouldn't take him long to ascertain her ignorance on the all-important meaning of that painting.

'No. Not long,' she prevaricated. 'But I'm not inclined to let it go, Mr Eastern. It has... a personal value... to me.' She studied him carefully as she added, 'I wondered if it had a personal value to you, over and above your art collecting.'

He pasted an indulgent smile on his lips. 'I only saw it for the first time last night, Miss Hammond. I want it. That's about as personal as I ever feel about a painting.'

'I see,' she murmured, and went on eating. He wasn't about to crack. She had to apply more pressure, and there was only one way to do that. The same kind of pressure that had brought him to her breakfast table this morning.

She didn't drink any more champagne. She noticed he didn't touch his glass again either. He didn't return to the subject of the painting. He asked her how much she had seen of Australia, what she liked and disliked—a pleasantly innocuous conversation peppered by a flattering interest in her. Laura didn't believe in that interest for a moment. She merely played along with it until breakfast was over. Then she stood up and offered her hand.

'It's been quite fascinating meeting you, Mr Eastern. Thank you for your time.'

He rose from his chair, a tight, wary look flashing across his face as he took her hand. He held it. 'A pleasure, Miss Hammond. I trust you'll be instructing your agent to go ahead with the deal.'

A regretful little smile curved her lips. 'I'm sorry. I've decided not to sell.'

He was jolted all right! His fingers almost crushed hers. A bitter cynicism hardened his eyes. 'Miss Hammond, I don't really care to play games. I've never seen anyone walk away from a deal like the one I'm of-fering you. I don't believe you're doing this now.'

She held his gaze steadily; serene, confident, without so much as a flicker of movement on her face. 'Mr Eastern, I learnt to live without money or people a long time ago. I would be obliged if you'd release my hand.'

Frustration thinned his lips. Pure impotent fury stared back at her. He let her hand go. 'Why did you agree to meet me at all?' he rasped.

Laura didn't so much as flinch, answering with cool, calm logic. 'To discuss the painting. I'm afraid you didn't satisfy me as to the reason you wanted it. Think about that, Mr Eastern. Should you wish to discuss it further, you can contact me here. But the deadline is today!'

She could feel his eyes boring into her like laser beams as she walked away from him. It lent a heady exhil-aration to every step. Whether he came to her party or not, he certainly hadn't made a conquest of her. Un-doubtedly such an occurrence was a totally new ex-perience for him. Laura could not help grinning to herself over that little triumph. He had dismissed her last night. She had well and truly returned the compliment just now. In that respect they were even.

The first lift to arrive was going down, and she stepped into it without hesitation. Better to get away while the going was good. The doors closed sharply, but she had one brief view of Jared Eastern before he was shut out. He hadn't moved. He was still staring after her. And he didn't look the least bit defeated. In fact, Laura felt a most discomfiting sensation of danger, as if she had aroused a savage beast that would stalk her to the ends of the earth.

She tried to shrug it off as the lift descended to street-level, but she was forcefully reminded of her fanciful impressions of him last night—a warrior who dared any-thing, who let nothing stand in his way. She walked quickly through the foyer and asked the doorman to summon a taxi, instinctively choosing a fast getaway.

'Where to?' the driver asked.

The door was closed, the doorman already stepping back out of hearing range. 'Circular Quay,' she said quietly.

A ferry ride on Sydney Harbour seemed like a good idea. Any ferry would do. As long as she was safely out of reach for a while.

CHAPTER THREE

LAURA strolled along the quay checking ferry destinations and timetables. Her eye was caught by a poster advertising Taronga Park Zoo and she impulsively made her decision. The ferry departure clock told her she had ten minutes to wait. She shot a quick look along the tourist stalls which were set up near the piers, and spotted a stand of straw hats. If she was going to walk in the sun her skin needed protection. She had been through too much to carelessly invite damage on herself.

Jared Eastern's words floated into her mind—'tantalisingly beautiful'. She wondered if he really thought that. One thing was certain: it was a lot easier to be beautiful than to be ugly. Not that Laura considered her face particularly remarkable. She was simply grateful to be normal. And whenever she looked in a mirror all she really saw was the miracle of the laser treatment.

Passengers were streaming on to the ferry by the time she had made her purchase, and she hurried to join the tail-end of the queue. Once on board she chose to stay on the outside deck, not wanting to miss any part of the view. The trip across the harbour was a delight. Laura had no quarrel with the claim that it was the most magnificent harbour in the world. In all her travels she had never seen better. The myriad coves and inlets were packed with pleasure-boats and the traffic on the water was full of interest. She even managed to push Jared Eastern out of her mind for a while as her eyes darted around the foreshores, taking everything in.

As it turned out, Taronga Park Zoo was not a good choice for providing distraction from the man she had walked out on. The dangerous animals were in safe enclosures, but quite a few of them reminded her of Jared Eastern. He was not caged in any way whatsoever. Nor was he the kind of man who would ever accept being confined by anything. He would get back to her. The only question was what ammunition he would use at their next meeting.

Whatever he planned, Laura was not about to be swayed by anything but the truth. Jared Eastern knew what that painting meant, and he didn't like it. Not one bit. He didn't want to share that knowledge with her. Or with anyone else. Somehow she would have to force it out of him. The only ammunition she had was her relationship to the man who had painted *Lost Dreams*. Would that be enough to surprise Jared Eastern into revealing what she wanted to know?

Unlikely, she thought, but the challenge excited her. In fact, she had never met anyone of Jared Eastern's calibre before. She sensed he was a loner like her, and probably even more self-sufficient than she was. He would never hesitate about going anywhere by himself, but then he wasn't a woman. He was very emphatically a man—of a breed that Laura thought had all but been lost in the Western World.

He was clothed in sophisticated civilisation, but that didn't quite hide the innate savagery of his nature. He had no respect for women. He used them as he pleased. Laura had no doubt about that, yet she couldn't help wondering what it would be like to be taken by such a man. To feel the raw power of his body moving over her, surging inside her.

Laura shook her head. She didn't want to think of Jared Eastern, or the power of his attraction. Sex was hardly her number one priority. Three years ago she had been in love—or rather she had been in love with the idea of being in love. She had found out then that men could break a relationship in order to get on with their lives. And she was certain that Jared Eastern was in the same mould.

All the men she attracted were men of strength. She wondered if it was a weakness in her own character that drew them to her. Even a person like Steven Hershaw—on the surface charming and cultured, but that was a social veneer. He was like all the others, with an inner purpose and a ruthless power to batter their way over every obstacle to reach their goal at the top.

There must be something wrong with her. To have a permanent relationship with people like that—it just wasn't on! They would have their wives when they were ready—and their mistresses on the side—but only their own lives counted for anything.

Yet there was something more about Jared Eastern, as if he would always stand astride everything else. She couldn't imagine him changing his values to fit into any conventional image. It was far more probable that he would change the convention to fit in with him. But that aspect of his character hardly explained why she had suddenly found herself considering him in a sexual sense.

It wasn't like her. She had only ever had the one lover, and she hadn't been bothered with such thoughts since that relationship had ended three years ago. Even with Tony it had not been easy for her to commit herself physically, wary of only being wanted as a body and not as the person she was. And the end result of their relationship had hurt so badly that she was doubly wary of repeating the experience. Yet there was something about Jared Eastern, some chemistry he stirred that made her extremely aware of being a woman . . . a woman with needs that had never been really answered. Or satisfied.

It was difficult to quell the feeling, particularly in his presence. Nevertheless, it had to be ignored throughout her next meeting with him. Not only ignored, but scrupulously hidden. She had no delusions about the man. If she showed any weakness, he would exploit it without a qualm.

But what if...?

A lion roared at her and Laura told herself she was utterly mad to be thinking such thoughts. She would probably be torn to pieces by a man such as Jared Eastern. She took herself off to the cafeteria for lunch, then wandered back down the path to the aquarium. Looking at sharks somehow reminded her again of the man she had challenged this morning, and she continued on to the ferry landing, deciding she had spent enough time away from the hotel. Maybe there would be a message waiting for her.

Again she stood at the railing as the ferry churned across the harbour. She took off her straw hat and the breeze ruffled through her hair like a lover's hand. The water danced with sunlit streaked waves. It felt good to be alive. And if Jared Eastern gave her the chance to be his lover—well, she wasn't making any decision now. But she had never felt so attracted to a man. And if she was to mess up her life, it was her life and no one else's. Where was she going anyway? What did it matter?

It was late afternoon by the time Laura got back to her hotel. Although there was a message from Jeremy Bursell, asking her to call him, she did not do so. She didn't want any hassling about the deal. While there was no word from Jared Eastern yet, Laura was certain he would make contact before the day was over.

She had the inner conviction that the Jared Easterns of this world didn't take kindly to losing a deal. And certainly not this one! When his response came, the pressure would be intense, and she had to be ready to cope with it. If nothing else, she intended to earn his respect!

The telephone call came at precisely five-thirty, and she identified his voice even before he gave his name. He wasted no time in getting to the point.

'You must allow me to return the compliment of a meal, Miss Hammond. Share dinner with me tonight.'

'Thank you, Mr Eastern. And I'll buy the champagne.'

'Hardly worthwhile. You barely tasted a drop this morning,' he said drily.

'Neither did you,' she reminded him.

He gave a low, throaty laugh. 'I look forward to meeting you again. I'll call you at seven o'clock, if that's convenient.'

'Fine! There's a lounge-bar beside the restaurant——'

'I think not. The places where one has tasted defeat should never be revisited, Miss Hammond. My choice of venue this time. I'll see you at seven.'

He hung up before she could ask where he meant to take her. Battle was rejoined. Laura was disconcerted to find her pulse racing. She wondered if she stimulated Jared Eastern in the same way he stimulated her, then decided that thinking in this manner was decidedly dangerous. She had to find out what he knew about the painting before ... well, before anything else.

She took a shower and spent a long time washing her hair. Having blow-dried it into shiny smoothness, Laura looked through her limited travel wardrobe and decided on the pink and white trouser-suit. It was made of a soft, silky, uncrushable fabric and was dressy enough or casual enough to cover most entertainment situations. It was also comfortable.

The long tunic top had loose three-quarter-length sleeves edged with a white embroidery pattern, as was the V-neckline. The outfit included a long sash in the same fabric. This could be tied around the waist or hung around the hips, but Laura chose to tie back her hair with it and let the ends dangle down her back. She thought it wiser not to accentuate any feminine curves tonight. She slipped her feet into high-heeled white sandals, and the only make-up she applied was a light pink lipstick. No jewellery. No perfume. Tonight was strictly business, she told herself. And today ran out at midnight. So something had to be settled by then.

At precisely seven o'clock the knock came on her door. Laura didn't keep him waiting. She paused only to pick up the white handbag she had prepared and to take a deep, calming breath. Which was just as well, or she might not have had any air in her lungs for some time after she opened the door.

Jared Eastern was dressed in a formal black dinner suit. He looked so devastatingly handsome, Laura felt as though she had been kicked in the heart. It was fortunate that she had long ago disciplined herself not to show any obvious reaction to people, because when he smiled it was extremely hard to keep a straight, unresponsive face. She allowed herself a small, polite smile.

'Pink suits you,' he said.

'Thank you,' she managed.

He held out his arm, and after a brief hesitation Laura took it and they walked down the corridor to the lifts. The muscled forearm under his coat-sleeve was rock-hard, and Laura noticed that the top of her head was level with his mouth. Which put him a couple of inches taller than six feet.

'You didn't say where we were going for dinner,' she remarked questioningly as they rode down to street-level.

His mouth quirked teasingly. 'You're such a difficult person to impress, Miss Hammond, I decided on somewhere uniquely special. I think you owe me one surprise.'

His suit suggested a high-class restaurant so Laura decided she had nothing to worry about. Besides, she had enough money in her handbag to cover any taxi-charge should she want to leave him.

He had not driven a car. They took a taxi and she had to share the back seat with him. Instead of stating a destination, Jared handed the driver a card, then settled back beside her and claimed her attention with conversation.

'Did you have a pleasant day?'

'Yes. Very relaxing,' she replied, noting that the car was heading down towards Circular Quay.

'Didn't you do anything exciting?'

She slanted him a dry look. 'I went to Taronga Park Zoo and talked to the animals.'

He gave the low, throaty laugh which was somehow very sexy. 'And what did the koalas and kangaroos say to you?'

'I thought it was probably more profitable to practise communicating with lions and tigers,' she said, then regretted the retort when he did not laugh again. The man was altogether too self-contained for her peace of mind.

'I don't believe in caging anything,' he said seriously. 'In fact, I hate it. I prefer to see animals in the wild where they belong.'

Laura turned her face away as she felt a discomfiting surge of heat tingle over her skin. Intuitively she knew that what he had said was true. He would open all the cages and let all the animals go free, as nature intended. She felt as though she had been reproved, but that was silly. She had to get her mind steeled to handle this encounter to the best of her ability. She noticed the car was still heading for the quay.

'How did you spend your day?' she asked, diverting his attention from cages.

'I took your advice and thought. I've had a very hard time of it.'

She darted a glance at him and found him smiling at her. 'I hope your thoughts were fruitful,' she said lightly.

'Not exactly. More like seeds in the wind. But we'll see where they blow tonight.'

Something glinted in his eyes and Laura once more felt a *frisson* of danger run down her spine. She tried to dismiss it, but it didn't help when the taxi pulled up outside a skyscraper office building. Jared Eastern was out and handing the driver his fare before Laura had time to ask questions. As soon as she alighted, he grasped her elbow and steered her towards the huge glass entrance doors. From inside a security guard moved to unlock them and hold one open.

'Good evening, Mr Eastern,' he greeted politely.

'Thanks, Daniel,' Jared returned, and steered Laura to a lift which he opened with a key.

Laura didn't want to step inside when the doors opened, yet she couldn't afford to show hesitation. That was the way of weakness. There was only one button to press and at Jared Eastern's jabbed command the lift sped upwards. Either they were going to a very exclusive night-spot at the top of the building, or she was being hijacked until further notice, Laura decided, and did her utmost to keep calm.

But fear was mounting in her. She had no idea how Jared Eastern was going to open the assault, but obviously he had something on his mind. There was no easy smile softening the determined set of his mouth now.

When she was ushered into a luxurious penthouse apartment with panoramic views of Sydney Harbour, Laura could have kicked herself for not anticipating it. He wouldn't want other people around them. And this way he not only kept his privacy but it allowed him to control the progress of their negotiations. Her riposte to it was quite obvious. She had to display complete unconcern.

'How lovely!' she said, moving across a spacious lounge-room to the largest picture-window. 'If this is your place, Mr Eastern, you certainly do yourself proud.'

'It's mine. And I work very hard for what I have, Miss Hammond,' he said, and there was a sharp edge to his voice. 'It would be extremely wise of you not to overlook that factor in your calculations.'

Laura slanted him a mocking look. 'Work is the arena of life to men like you, Mr Eastern. There's always another kill to be made in the market-place, isn't there? Something to beat...something to make your own. Always another horizon...another challenge. No, I don't overlook that,' she added quietly, and turned her gaze back to the view. 'I wonder how often you stop to look at what you have!'

He was reflected quite clearly in the window and Laura watched him surreptitiously, hoping she had struck a nerve that would rattle his arrogant confidence.

The muscles along his jawline tightened.

Laura smiled to herself. Body language could be very revealing, particularly when a person thought himself unobserved. She sensed that whatever he said next would be very important and she concentrated hard on listening to every nuance of meaning in the words.

'The point in question is...what are you after? What do you want?'

He bit out the words, still grimly controlling himself. Laura didn't reply. There was something else on his mind...something he was almost bursting to say...and she wanted him to say it. Yet when it came, what he said was so surprising that she would never have been prepared for it. His mouth curled and he delivered the words with hard, stinging mockery.

'Let's go straight to the heart of the matter, Miss Hammond. Only it's not Miss Hammond, is it? It's Miss McKenzie. The daughter of Andrew McKenzie!'

CHAPTER FOUR

LAURA kept very still until her heart stopped misbehaving itself. Jared Eastern had taken the surprise element from her and used it himself, but that needn't work against her. Not if she kept her wits. She turned slowly, the grey eyes clear and steady.

'My name *is* Hammond. I was legally adopted by my mother's second husband. But my real father was Andrew McKenzie,' she stated evenly, then gave him a dry smile. 'You have been busy...to find that out in one day.' She almost added that it had taken nearly her entire lifetime to get that critical piece of information, but she held her tongue, hoping to hear what it meant to him.

His grim expression was unrelieved, mercilessly hard. 'It wasn't too difficult to find out from Jeremy Bursell. He likes money, and a lot of it. You should have given him instructions to keep your identity a secret.'

She shrugged. 'There was no point to it. I was going to tell you anyway. Sooner or later.'

'Yes. Of course. It had to come out, didn't it? You must have been cock-a-hoop last night when I took the bait. And this morning you dragged me right in. But tonight...' His eyes gleamed with unrelenting satisfaction. 'Tonight we are going to get this thing settled. One way or another. Once and for all. For the rest of eternity!'

Laura had no idea what he was talking about. Although she had hoped the painting would bring something to light about her father's past, and Jared's reaction was suggestive of something highly important to him, she was still totally ignorant of the issue involved. Somehow she had to keep provoking him to do the talking.

'I'm not averse to getting everything settled tonight,' she said lightly. 'That would suit me very well.'

His mouth curled sardonically. 'Then perhaps we're thinking along the same lines.'

'Mmm...perhaps,' she said non-committally, then with cool deliberation she moved her gaze to the paintings on the wall behind him.

They were expertly lit and provided the only colour in a room whose other furnishings were all black and white and starkly modern. Having studied the works of the other Australian artists on exhibition in the art gallery, Laura was able to identify a Drysdale, a Sidney Nolan, and a Pro Hart, all originals and very definitely collector's pieces.

'You have a fine taste in art,' she commented.

When he didn't answer she turned her gaze back to him, one eyebrow lifted enquiringly.

The green eyes glittered at her in mocking appreciation. 'I'll say this for you. You've got nerves of steel.'

He walked slowly towards her, each step testing her composure. Laura suddenly knew what it felt like to be an animal mesmerised by fear. She could not tear her eyes from his, and her heart seemed to be thundering in her ears. But he wouldn't really threaten her physically, she reasoned frantically. That would be beneath his pride.

He stopped a bare half-pace away from her and his hand lifted to her cheek. His fingertips brushed lightly over her skin as he spoke softly, his words almost as hypnotic as his actions. 'It's not that I don't appreciate what you've been through. I do. I even have a certain grudging admiration for the way you've gone about it. And I'm prepared to reach a compromise. There always is a compromise to be reached with people like you and me, isn't there?'

What was he talking about? Was he serious, or was he playing with her, intent on getting through her guard by any means at all? Laura could not trust him. And, as if he read the scepticism that dampened the power he was exerting, the glitter in his eyes grew taunting.

'Perhaps not,' he said in mocking challenge.

It was an act of sheer will-power to force her voice into a cool, crisp tone. 'What do you want, Mr Eastern?'

'Right at this moment, Laura McKenzie-Hammond, I'm not sure whether to hate you...or kiss you senseless.'

Laura had an awful suspicion he was quite capable of doing both—particularly the latter. 'Perhaps at this juncture, not at all wise,' she said drily. Not through any intention. Her mouth had lost all moisture.

'Perhaps something in between,' he agreed, then broke the tension with a sardonic smile. 'I wasn't sure whether you were going to throw your arms around my neck and try to kiss *me* senseless, or get down on your knees and beg. So I wanted to find out.'

'I'm afraid that neither response entered my mind,' Laura said truthfully.

The low laugh gravelled from his throat as his finger-tips grazed down over her lips to her chin, leaving a trace of shivery sensation in their wake. Again it took an enormous concentration of will-power for Laura to keep absolutely still. At least on the outside. She had no control whatsoever on the wild, churning inside.

Her effort was rewarded by the admiration that crept into his eyes. She felt almost dizzy with exultation at this unconcealed evidence of respect in such a formidable opponent.

'You'll do fine,' he said enigmatically. 'Just fine.'

She sensed she had won a victory, that he had just conceded something important, but what it was she had no idea. Nevertheless, the more he said, the more intriguing and tantalising the mystery became, and Laura silently determined not to give her position away, no matter what! All she had to do was wait, and eventually she would find out what the victory entailed.

'Perhaps you'll do fine too,' she said, resolved on matching his game without conceding a thing.

Something decidedly feral and dangerous lit his eyes for a fleeting second. Then he withdrew a pace and took her hand. 'So let's get down to business,' he said, and drew her over to one of the white leather sofas arranged around a low glass coffee-table.

Apparently Jared did mean to serve her some food and drink. On the table were set a tray of hors-d'oeuvres, two very elegant glasses, and a silver ice-bucket which was chilling a bottle of champagne. He saw her seated then gave his attention to the champagne. He said nothing until he had poured the wine and placed a glass within easy hand-reach. Then he waved an invitation for her to help to help herself to the hors-d'oeuvres.

'I recommend the caviare. It's Beluga, which is more to my personal taste than Sevruga.'

'Thank you,' Laura murmured. She carefully spread some on to a crouton and took a bite, needing something to settle her stomach.

Jared settled on to the sofa opposite and sipped his glass of champagne, his eyes boring into her with unwavering intensity. 'You are gambling, you know,' he drawled. 'I don't believe I have any liability or responsibility in this matter. It may not be worth your while to go on with what you've started.'

Laura didn't believe him. She wasn't gambling. Not any more. The only trouble was, she didn't know what she was talking about. 'Mmm...don't you think we are all victims of our own opinions?' she offered, hoping the comment fitted well enough.

'Why not just walk away with a clear five million?' he retorted.

She shook her head. 'For most people five million dollars is a dream. But I can't accept it. There's a trust involved—a trust I mean to keep, however stupid it may appear to anyone else. And secondly, it's not what I want.'

His mouth took on a cynical twist. 'It's up to you to propose,' he said. 'And I'll accept.'

Laura's mind whirled to no effect. She didn't know what proposition to make. She picked up her glass of champagne and sipped it as she mulled over the problem. The only solution to the impasse was not to propose anything at all.

Her eyes flicked up to meet his in bold challenge. 'You propose. And I'll think about it.'

Her response seemed to take his breath away. 'You're totally ruthless!' he bit out.

'In this matter, yes,' Laura said fearlessly, hoping the extra pressure might open him up.

The green eyes spent several fraught moments fiercely reassessing her. 'There is no other settlement you will make?'

'None!' she declared, feeling a heady recklessness with this mad game of feeding him lines.

He stared at her as if he couldn't quite believe her stance. Laura put down her glass and selected a small pastry-boat filled with creamed crab-meat from the tray. She ate it with relish. Being with Jared Eastern seemed to sharpen all her senses.

'Have you considered *all* the options?' he demanded more than asked.

She flicked a glance at him. He was frowning heavily. She smiled. 'All I can think of,' she replied truthfully. It was really quite marvellous how he was taking this all so seriously when she didn't have a clue what they were on about. At the moment, she definitely had the upper hand. *He* was worried.

'And that's your final position?'

'It appears to be.' She was getting quite good at this double-talk. It was now sliding right off the top of her head. She took another drink to show how relaxed she was.

'I won't say I haven't considered it. As a last resort.'

His eyes probed hers for some crack in her armour. Laura whimsically decided that ignorance was bliss in this instance. She didn't bat an eyelid.

'I thought you would back away from it,' he said testingly.

Laura simply stared back, using silence as a prod for more elaboration.

His mouth curled. 'It certainly saves on litigation . . . and does away with any adverse publicity.' He seemed to be convincing himself.

Laura kept silent, turning his words over in her mind. She wondered what legal action he thought she might have against him. She was quite certain they weren't talking about the painting any more. It had to be about the diamond mine.

Maybe her father had once had a legal claim on it. He might also have had a moral claim on it. Either way, Jared Eastern was foreseeing bad publicity if she fought him in the courts. In her present state of ignorance, Laura knew she didn't have a hope of winning anything, but there was no doubt Jared was taking the matter very very seriously. The five million dollars was testament to that!

'I don't think I could stand it if you were frigid,' he said menacingly.

'I don't think I would be.'

The words slipped out before Laura could catch them back. She had been so preoccupied with trying to figure out the situation that she had made an automatic response without stopping to take in the meaning of what Jared had said. Her mind seized up entirely when it finally locked on to the word 'frigid' and she stared uncomprehendingly at Jared as he rose to his feet, his powerful body emanating ruthless purpose.

'You've played Little Miss Cool all the way to this position,' he said grimly. 'So let's check that out.'

Laura was still struggling to understand as he stepped around the table, took the glass of champagne from her hand, set it down, and pulled her up from the sofa. What did her being frigid or not have to do with anything? She certainly didn't feel the least bit frigid as he drew her slowly into an embrace that made her overwhelmingly aware of his hard masculinity. Heat raced around her veins. And when he bent his head to claim her lips with his, they quivered with an electric response.

He began a very controlled sensual assault on her mouth which Laura found too fascinating to resist. As much as it might weaken her position—whatever that was—she had been wondering all day what Jared Eastern might be like as a lover, and she was not about to pass up the opportunity to find out. In a limited way, of course.

She slid her arms up around his neck, deliberately encouraging a deepening of the kiss. Whether he was surprised by her initiative or not, he took immediate advantage of it. Afterwards Laura didn't quite know what it was that triggered pleasant excitement into something else, but suddenly there was no more testing or conscious deliberation. Something exploded between them—a voracious desire for more and more sensation...possession...wild erotic intimacy...an uncontrollable urge to merge until there could be no separation.

And the separation when it came was brutally swift and violent. Jared wrenched his mouth from hers and threw back his head, his neck muscles so taut and strong that she could not bend them. She felt hurt, bewildered that he should want to end what had been happening between them. To her it had been the most sensational experience in her life, and her whole body craved for it to continue.

Her breasts were pressed so hard against him, they were deeply sensitive to the quick rise and fall of his chest, and a fierce elation ran through her as she belatedly registered the unmistakable pressure of male desire against the softness of her stomach. So he was not unaffected by her! He was fighting for control!

The realisation gave Laura an exhilarating sense of power. There was no way he could deny his reaction to her, so there was no triumph to be gleaned from her reaction to him. When he dropped his gaze to hers, she met it with a fearless pride that granted him nothing.

There was a guarded look in his eyes as he assessed the expression in hers. His mouth quirked in amused appreciation of her challenge. 'Well, the mind might be a steel-trap, but the body is all woman,' he commented.

'I didn't doubt that you were a man,' she retorted mockingly. 'But it's always reassuring to check.'

His low, throaty laugh denied any embarrassment over the proof of his virility. 'Consider the matter settled. When do you want the marriage to take place?'

Marriage! Laura didn't have a ready answer. She didn't know what answer to give. Her mind went into a double-loop, wheeling through all that had gone before in a frantic grasp for enlightenment. 'You...propose...and I'll accept'! And she had demanded that he propose! She hadn't meant marriage, but Jared obviously thought she had.

It was ridiculous! But how could she explain that? And he was waiting for her answer! She had fantasised about being his lover...but his wife? The idea had an instant and compelling appeal, and after that kiss she wasn't going to say no. Not yet anyway.

'What's convenient to you?' she countered, privately acknowledging that she had gone quite mad, but the last thing she wanted was to turn him off right at this moment.

'The sooner, the better, as far as I'm concerned. Then I can ensure that you don't get up to any funny business.' His eyes simmered into hers as he moved his hand sensuously down her back to the base of her spine, deliberately re-igniting the desire that had flared between them. 'Let's make it tomorrow.'

Why not? Laura thought recklessly. No other man had ever made her feel so sharply alive, both mentally and physically. Not even Tony. And she had once planned to marry him. Why not give it a chance with Jared Eastern? Excitement fevered her mind and, before cooler reason could prevail, she committed herself.

'Yes,' she said. 'I've got nothing better to do tomorrow.' Nothing better to do for the rest of her life, she argued to herself. And this would certainly be a change...for better or for worse. To hold a man like Jared Eastern could be the most stimulating challenge she could ever possibly have.

'We are agreed, then,' he said with satisfaction, and Laura felt a little quiver of uncertainty as the simmer of desire retreated into driving purpose. 'I'll make whatever arrangements are necessary.'

'That suits me,' she said with firm bravado. After all, if she changed her mind in the interim, she could always board a plane and be on her way back to Boston while he waited for her at the altar. But even at this stage she didn't think that was going to happen.

For the rest of the evening Laura wondered if she had taken leave of her senses. She had come here to find out about her father and been swept into a decision that she could never have anticipated in her wildest dreams. The realisation that she didn't have to go through with it steadied her nerves. And she further realised that Jared's acceptance of this mad marriage certainly told her something about her father. And his life.

How she was going to find out the actual facts, she didn't know. In her present position she could hardly confess to ignorance on the matter. But some things were obvious. Jared Eastern thought he owed her something—or, more to the point, owed her father something. And he was prepared to go as far as marriage to make reparation for whatever wrong had been done to her father in the past.

But their marriage was bound to be a bitter relationship with Jared thinking her a coldly calculating operator who was out to get all she could. On the other hand, he had been doing quite a bit of calculating himself—saving on litigation that he obviously thought would cost him dear. He couldn't consider her any more mercenary than he was. And he hadn't seemed displeased with the bargain they had struck. After she had proved she wasn't frigid.

That put them on level terms. He wasn't frigid either. And that was probably the only way any woman would ever get to be on level terms with Jared Eastern. The thought gave Laura a surprisingly deep satisfaction. She wouldn't be a mere female cipher in his life. She had the power—if she only knew what that power was— to blow his hard-worked-for world apart. And she didn't care if that was fair or not at this particular moment.

Nevertheless, a sense of unreality pervaded the ensuing conversation with him. Jared forged ahead, settling the practical details that their marriage entailed.

Laura said 'yes' to everything he suggested, from an un-ceremonious wedding to a dismissal of any pretence-form of a honeymoon. When he dictated that they fly to Bendeneer Downs the morning after their marriage, she didn't even enquire where that was, or what it was, as-senting without question, even though she noticed that her agreement brought a wicked gleam of satisfaction to his dark green eyes.

That did jerk her out of her introspection enough to recognise that Jared wasn't accepting this marriage with any good will towards her. He might find her desirable enough to bed for a while, but one way or another he was determined to beat her at the game he thought she was playing. She had a tiger by the tail at the moment. But no way would he ever be tamed. Oddly enough, she didn't feel the least bit put off by that thought. On the contrary, it excited her all the more. She really must be mad, Laura thought, or something was definitely wrong with her. Nevertheless, she kept playing along with him.

It was the telephone call that spelled the reality out to her in no uncertain terms. She and Jared had finished dinner and were back in the lounge-room drinking coffee when the call came. He frowned in irritation at the in-terruption, but he picked up the receiver from a side-table next to the sofa he occupied. He had kept out of any physical contact with her after that one testing kiss, and Laura watched him with absorbed interest from the opposite sofa as he curtly gave his name.

Naturally she could only hear his side of the conver-sation, but it served to focus her mind very sharply.

'No,' he said unequivocally. 'You'll have to handle it yourself, Rafe. I can't come. I have something more im-portant here.'

There was a brief silence as the caller apparently argued. Jared's mouth curled into a sardonic smile. 'I'm getting married tomorrow. As far as I'm concerned, that has top priority. Do whatever you think best. I'm not in the mood to care at this particular moment. My fiancée is with me.'

A cynical amusement danced in his eyes as he listened to the caller's reaction. Then… 'She's not an Australian. She's an American. From Boston, Massachusetts. And I don't intend to wait for anything, Rafe. This is my private business.'

Another question was obviously raised and Jared's eyes suddenly hardened as they lifted to meet Laura's questioning gaze and hold it with unrelenting purpose. 'Her name is Laura Hammond. But by tomorrow night it will be Laura Eastern. Laura and I are agreed that our marriage is a private matter between ourselves. And that is final, Rafe. I'll be in touch when I'm ready to be and not before.'

The receiver was decisively put down, ending any further argument. And it was at that moment that Laura made up her mind. Jared was committed to their marriage and she was not going to back out. However foolish it might prove to be, it was a gamble that had to be taken or she would always regret not knowing what they might have shared together, even if it was only the most primitive sharing-ground that existed between a man and a woman.

He took her back to her hotel and saw her up to her room. She had already handed him her passport to facilitate any legalities which were required in order to get married, and there was nothing she could think of to hold him with her any longer. She opened the door with her pass-card and paused to look up at him, half hoping he would kiss her goodnight to add even more conviction to her decision.

His expression was stern and somewhat forbidding, which made her wonder if he was having second thoughts about marrying her. She said, 'Goodnight' quickly, anxious to keep the status quo, but he stopped her as she would have stepped inside her room, his hand grasping her arm hard.

'One more thing, Laura,' he said, his eyes burning with commanding intensity. 'That painting is to be removed from the exhibition first thing in the morning. Get Bursell to store it. Replace it with something else. I don't care what arrangements you make, so long as it's never on public view again. Is that understood?'

The painting! Of course, she thought sadly. That was at the heart of everything...the goad that had driven Jared into the extraordinary moves that would see them married tomorrow. And she still didn't know what it meant!

His fingers dug bruisingly into her flesh and a flash of ferocity added bite to the command in his eyes. 'You're getting what you want. Now I get what I want. From here on in the fun and games are over. Don't doubt that for one second.'

She didn't. She made a mental note never to reveal to him how this situation had come about, not in any circumstances. 'I'll take care of it first thing in the morning,' she assured him unequivocally.

She had always felt guilty about putting the painting on exhibition anyhow, and now it had served its purpose. Not that she had all the answers she had been seeking, but she was quite confident that time would bring them to light. Jared's assumption that she already knew them was half the battle. It would all fall into place sooner or later.

Jared looked at her searchingly as if he wasn't quite sure he could trust her word. Then he nodded and released her arm. 'You're not a fool. I'll say that for you, Laura McKenzie-Hammond.' He touched her cheek in a mocking salute. 'Until tomorrow.'

Laura released her breath in a disappointed sigh as he strode off down the corridor. Obviously Jared was unwilling to concede anything else to her, although she had sensed he was tempted to kiss her in that moment before turning away. Perhaps tempted to do more than that. Had the possibility of losing his control made him think twice about it?

A proud, very self-contained man was Jared Eastern, Laura thought, but after tomorrow he would be her husband. He wouldn't turn away then.

A little smile of absolute satisfaction curved Laura's mouth as she stepped inside her room and closed the door. Tomorrow would come soon enough.

CHAPTER FIVE

LAURA had two telephone-calls to make the next morning. She dealt with business first.

'You sold it!' Jeremy Bursell's voice rose in excitement as he leapt to the conclusion suggested by her request.

'No. I'll never sell it, Jeremy. I simply want it taken out of the exhibition,' Laura said evenly. 'I've decided I don't want it shown any more, so I'd be grateful if you'd store it for me until further notice.'

'But——' He sounded perplexed.

Laura swept on. 'The painting my father did of the Daintree rain-forest is the same size, and the title of *Lost Dreams* could apply to it equally well. If you hang that in the gallery, it will fill the space and no one will raise questions about it.'

'But...' The dealer in fine arts was beginning to sound like a broken record. 'But surely you sold it?'

'I believe you did some profitable business with Jared Eastern yesterday,' Laura reminded him drily. 'And no, I didn't sell it.'

There was a short silence. Jeremy Bursell was far from being a fool and Laura could imagine the calculating wheels of his mind furiously clicking through all sorts of possible sequences. When he spoke it was with wary circumspection. 'How did you know about yesterday?'

Laura smiled. There would be no more argument about the painting. And the fine arts dealer would be a lot more circumspect about *her* business in future. She pitched a light tone into her reply.

'Jeremy, you talk too much. What you told Jared Eastern was indiscreet, to say the least. But I'm a very forgiving person. I'll overlook it this time. All you're losing is the commission on five million dollars. On the other hand, Jared Eastern has a fine art collection, and over the years he may very well buy a lot more paintings from you. You've made a good contact there, Jeremy.'

She paused, then pushed home the punchline. 'You will see to this matter of replacing the painting this morning, won't you? As far as I'm concerned it can't be done soon enough.'

She heard the expulsion of breath on the other end of the line. 'Certainly... certainly! I'll get moving on it straight away.'

'Thank you, Jeremy. I appreciate it. You're a fine agent.'

Manipulation was certainly the name of the game, Laura thought as she hung up. Know enough about a person and the moves became obvious. Jeremy Bursell was well aware that he had committed an indiscretion yesterday, and he didn't want to lose her business.

Laura heaved a sigh as she placed her next call. Her mother would never forgive her if she got married without telling her. It was bad enough that the wedding wouldn't be a huge society affair in Boston. It would be much worse if Laura didn't give her the courtesy of some forewarning, although the short notice made it impossible for Connie and Ted Hammond to put in an attendance. Which was just as well, Laura thought gratefully. The situation was tricky enough as it was.

'You're marrying an Australian?' Connie Hammond's shock and disapproval could not have been clearer if she had been standing right in front of her wayward daughter. 'I knew that no good would come of going back there,' was the first tight-lipped comment.

Laura offered the kind of consolation that might best appease her mother. 'Jared is the most striking-looking man you could ever imagine, Mother.'

'So was your father,' was the terse condemnation.

And that was news to Laura! It certainly answered how her mother had come to make 'her mistake'. Good looks were almost everything to Connie Hammond. Her own daughter's disfigurement had been close to unbearable for her. It was an attitude of mind that had added immeasurably to Laura's inner pain. However, now was not the time to nag over old hurts. She pressed on with her next favourable point.

'He's also fabulously wealthy.'

'What from?'

Old money or new, she meant, and the innate snobbery of that question made Laura bridle. But nothing was ever going to change her mother's attitudes, and at least she wouldn't be able to find some unfashionable taint about the answer.

'Diamonds, Mother. I don't know if you've ever heard of the Kimberley coloured diamonds, but they're the finest in the world, and Jared mines them. As far as eligible bachelors go, I'd say he's probably King of the Roost.'

'Don't be vulgar, Laura.' There was a slight pause, then grudgingly, 'I suppose he might be acceptable.'

'I'm accepting him anyway,' Laura said testily.

'Yes. Well, I suppose I should be grateful you're telling me at all,' her mother said disparagingly. 'And why all the haste? I don't like this. Are you telling me all the truth?'

'Mother!'

'Well, why aren't you getting married properly?'

Laura sighed. Her mother's fears were natural enough in the light of her own 'mistake'. 'I'm not pregnant, Mother. Quite simply, Jared doesn't want to wait.'

'Women make men wait. It isn't proper——'

'Mother! I'm getting married today. Please accept that!'

There was a short silence after Laura's sharp interjection. Then frosty resignation. 'I expect Ted can get a dossier on this Jared Eastern so that we can release the news here. But I would be obliged—if it's not too much trouble—if you would send me a photograph of the wedding. I doubt it will make the society pages...'

'I doubt that Jared would like the publicity anyway.'

'Laura, I don't understand you.'

'I don't think I understand myself.' And that was true enough in this instance, Laura thought, although her mother would never appreciate the point.

A heavy sigh hissed over the line. 'When are we going to meet him?'

'I'll let you know in good time, Mother. We're flying to Bendeneer Downs tomorrow. I'll give you our full address when I write.'

'Laura...' Suddenly there was a different, more urgent tone to her mother's voice. 'Laura...' It sounded as if she was swallowing. 'How long have you known this man?'

'Long enough to know that I want to marry him, Mother. Please don't worry. I promise you——'

'Laura, that's no answer. You're evading...' There was a shuddering breath then, 'Laura, I had only known your father for four hours when I...I fell madly in love with him. And for all we felt for each other, it turned out to be a terrible mistake. We didn't know each other well enough. Believe me, I know how strong physical attraction can be. But, my dear——'

'Mom...' Strange, she hadn't called her mother that in years. Yet she couldn't remember the last time she had heard such deep caring in her voice. Tears pricked at Laura's eyes. 'It's more than that. Truly. I'm not as young as you were, Mom. Please...just wish me luck.'

'You won't wait?' Her voice quavered slightly.

'No,' Laura said softly.

'I wish...I do wish you luck, Laura. We don't ever seem to communicate very well, but I've always wanted the best for you. You do know that, don't you?'

'Yes. Yes, of course I do, Mom.' The lump in her throat was getting difficult to circumvent. It seemed silly to feel so emotional and yet...maybe there was something about getting married that brought mothers and daughters closer together no matter how great the distance. It wasn't anyone's fault that they had different values. Different things shaped different lives. And by her own lights her mother had done her best for her. 'Thank you,' she managed huskily. 'Thank you for all you've done for me.'

'Laura...' There was a heavy sigh. 'I do hope you know what you're doing.'

'So do I,' Laura breathed, then steadied her voice. 'I must go now, Mom. I'll be in touch again real soon.'

It was a relief to end the call. She hadn't expected it to upset her. Probably when they met again she and her mother would revert to their old fencing ways...poles apart. But it had been good—if it was only ever this one time—to be reassured that she wasn't just a show-daughter to her mother, that there was a very real caring underneath it all.

Nevertheless, it would have been impossible to make her mother understand her decision. Laura did indeed hope she knew what she was doing, but somehow it no longer mattered if she did or not. One thing she did know. She wasn't marrying Jared Eastern for his looks or his wealth. Nor for what he could tell her about her father. It was something far more basic than that. Something in the nature of the man which drew her irresistibly to meet the challenge he threw out.

She wiped her eyes and took a deep breath. One thing she could do to please her mother was to do as she asked and have a photograph taken of the wedding. And be dressed in a manner that would meet her approval. Since she wouldn't be hearing from Jared until early afternoon, she had plenty of time to go shopping for a wedding outfit. Something really special. After all, getting married was a special occasion in one's life, however unusual the arrangement. And even if their marriage was a terrible mistake, Laura couldn't imagine herself ever getting married again. She suspected that all other men would pale when matched against Jared Eastern.

She thoroughly enjoyed the morning, browsing through three bridal salons before finding what she wanted. Although she had been tempted by several rather romantic dresses, the thought of the cynical amusement they might spark in Jared's green eyes was enough to put her off them. But the white silk suit was perfect: simple, elegant, and wickedly expensive.

The classic form-fitting style made the most of her curvaceous figure, and both the coat and the skirt couldn't have fitted better if she'd had them made personally for her. There was a saucy little hat to go with the suit, made of the same silk. It sat beautifully over the crown of her head and featured a stiff little ruffle which tapered down one side to just below her ear. She splurged all the way with shoes and a clutch handbag to match, and finally returned to the hotel feeling exhilarated with her purchases. She spread them out on the bed to take pleasure in looking at them, then ordered a light lunch from room-service.

No sooner had she put the telephone down than it started buzzing. She picked it up again and was surprised that it was Jared calling, much earlier than they had arranged.

'I've been trying to get you all morning,' he started in a curt tone.

'I had the painting taken out of the exhibition,' she returned with equal curtness.

'I know that. I wanted to check if you need any help... need any clothes...'

'I'm fine, thank you.'

The tone gathered a sardonic edge. 'I thought you would be well organised. I expected nothing less.'

'You can back out any time you like, Jared,' Laura challenged.

'Three hours to countdown,' he said grimly. 'And it's all systems go.'

'Fine!' Laura bit off crisply.

'Unfortunately we have an extra problem to take care of. My mother is demanding to meet you. She arrived this morning. As my bride-to-be you have to look the part. I trust your wardrobe covers that contingency?'

So that was why he had been trying to reach her! Laura smiled. His problem made it easy to settle her problem. 'My mother is demanding something too, Jared. A wedding photograph. I bought a suitable outfit this morning. Will you arrange a photographer or shall I?'

He muttered something under his breath before answering. 'Leave it to me. Can you be dressed and ready by two o'clock?'

'Certainly.'

'I have our head jeweller flying in from Perth. With the appropriate adornment for a bride of diamonds. I'm sure you'll appreciate the point,' he drawled cynically. 'If all goes well, I'll bring him to your room at two o'clock. Some pieces might need adjustment.'

'As you wish,' she replied shortly. Diamonds meant nothing to her, but there was no longer any doubt that they were the whole basis of this marriage, so she couldn't disillusion Jared on that score.

'Little Miss Cool,' he said derisively. 'Have you any idea how provocative...? No, don't bother answering that. I'm sure you know exactly what you're doing.'

The line was abruptly disconnected.

Laura could not help grinning to herself as she put the receiver down. Jared had slipped up, revealing that he found her façade of cool control provocative. Maybe she got to him in the same way he got to her. And if that was so... well, she might be a bride of diamonds, but she would be a wife that Jared Eastern wouldn't find it easy to shrug off in a hurry.

Laura almost danced around the room as she effected most of her packing, and her inner excitement robbed her of much of her appetite when her lunch was delivered. She picked over enough of the ham salad to keep hunger at bay, then set the room-service tray outside her door to be collected, glad to have the ordered meal out of the way. Reason whispered that her exhilarating sense of anticipation was totally unmerited in these circumstances, but she took great pleasure in getting ready for her wedding.

She was showered, manicured, perfumed and dressed by five minutes to two. All that remained to be done was to put on her hat, and she decided that could wait until after the jeweller's visit. She had coiled the thick mass of her hair into a neat chignon just above the nape of her neck and she had tried the hat on to ensure that it still sat neatly over her crown. She had even gone to the trouble of applying some subtle make-up to her eyes, mindful of the photograph her mother expected, and, while Laura was not over-endowed with feminine vanity, she thought she looked as good as she could look.

Certainly Jared's eyes glinted with satisfaction when she opened the door to his knock. Her heart gave an exultant leap and it was all she could do to keep her lips restricted to a polite smile. And wrench her eyes off her husband-to-be to take in the man who accompanied him. He was small and well past middle-age, his shoulders slightly stooped, his hair completely grey. But his eyes were sharp with curiosity as they appraised Laura.

'Harold Stern, Laura,' Jared quickly introduced. 'May we come in?'

'How do you do, Mr Stern?' Laura offered her hand, and the man quickly transferred the briefcase he held so that he could oblige her.

'A pleasure to meet you, Miss Hammond,' he said with a twinkling smile.

Jared made a sound of impatience. Laura cast him a reproving look, although her pulse was still racing at the sight of him. He was superbly turned out in a light grey suit that had an air of formality about it, particularly with the silver-grey satin tie that sat on his white silk shirt. Having made Jared wait a few moments—as her mother would have approved—she stood back and waved the two men inside her room.

Harold Stern headed straight for the desk under the mirror. He set the flat briefcase on it and proceeded to open its various locks.

Jared paused beside Laura, the green eyes alight with mocking appreciation. 'You've won Mr Stern over,' he said in a low voice. 'But then you're very good at winning, aren't you?'

'I know what it's like to be a loser. I didn't find it an enjoyable experience,' she tossed back, then walked down the room to where the jeweller had opened his case.

'Do you know your ring size, Miss Hammond?' the little man asked.

'No, Mr Stern. I'm afraid not.'

'May I have your left hand, please?'

He tried a series of rings on her third finger until he was satisfied with a fitting. He glanced up at her earlobes, noting the tiny gold studs she wore as sleepers. 'They are pierced. Good! There'll be no trouble there.'

He handed a box to Jared. 'The earrings,' he murmured. Then he lifted another box from his case and opened it without any ceremony. Laura's incredulous gasp brought a delighted smile to the little man's face. 'The Eastern Star,' he told her proudly.

The pendant was indeed designed as a star with brilliant baguette diamonds radiating from the centrepiece which was one single stone, its size and the predominantly pink colour totally breathtaking.

Jared watched assessingly as the jeweller fastened the fine platinum chain around her neck. 'Needs to be taken up a bit,' he instructed, then nodded. 'Yes. That's perfect.'

The pendant was removed from her throat and repacked in the jeweller's case which was promptly relocked. 'It won't take long, Jared,' Harold Stern informed him confidently.

'Good! We'll be here,' Jared replied, and ushered the little man out of the room.

Laura tried to regather some composure while Jared's back was still turned to her. There wasn't anything in the Hammond family jewellery that could remotely match the Eastern Star. She doubted that there was anything to match it anywhere, except possibly among the crown jewels of England. It made her nervous to even think about wearing it, let alone owning it! She had told her mother that Jared was fabulously wealthy. That pink diamond alone had to be worth tens of millions!

'Satisfied?' Jared mocked as he strolled back to her.

'It's very lovely,' Laura said stiffly.

His mouth curled. 'It's unique, Laura. As I'm damned sure you appreciate. And the ring and earrings are designed to match. There won't be a woman in the world who doesn't envy you them.'

He lifted a hand and lightly caressed the hollow of her throat with one tantalising finger. Laura found it difficult to keep breathing normally and she hoped he couldn't feel the leap in her pulse-rate.

'At least you have the kind of beauty that will set them off,' he said sardonically. The finger ran slowly up to her chin, tilting it slightly. His gaze dropped to her mouth. Her nerves started quivering in anticipation. But then his mouth thinned grimly and his eyes flicked up again, burning into hers with fierce determination. 'You are satisfied, I hope?'

'Completely,' Laura assured him.

'And needless to say, since we're agreed on this route to settle the issue between us, I don't want my mother to know you're Andrew McKenzie's daughter,' he stated coldly. 'You are Laura Hammond from Boston, Massachusetts, and we leave the pain of the past in the past. Forever, Laura. If that's not understood, I'm paying too much... and you will have done too little for your share.'

So there had been pain on both sides, Laura thought, not only on her father's. But that was not important right now.

'As you said last night, I'm not a fool,' she reminded him. 'And I do have integrity.'

Cold green eyes searched hers assessingly. 'I wouldn't have thought so,' he said slowly. 'But there is certainly going to come a time when we all find out.'

'You'll find out,' she said with conviction.

There was no point in telling him that she had never intended hurting anyone. If she ever showed any weakness he would walk right over her. If he ever found out what he'd done to himself... he would probably kill her!

Satisfaction took the chill out of his eyes. 'Would it be asking too much...do you think you can pretend to be madly in love with me? For my mother's benefit? I'd rather make her happy than unhappy.'

'As long as you can pretend for my mother. A few camera shots of wedded bliss? Do you think you can cope with it?' she countered mockingly.

He raised his eyebrows. 'She doesn't know what you're up to?'

'From what you've just asked me, no more than your mother does,' Laura retorted swiftly. 'Mine hates to be reminded of her first marriage. It pains her to even mention my father's name.'

'So...we embark on a mammoth deception together.' He gave his low, throaty laugh. 'At least it shouldn't be boring.'

'Precisely what I thought,' she returned, covering her inner exhilaration with a dry smile.

Again his gaze dropped to her mouth, fastened on it for several seconds, and Laura fiercely hoped he would kiss her. He wanted to. She was sure of it. But he dropped his hand, picked up hers, and almost slapped the box he had been holding in his other hand on to her palm.

'The earrings. You might as well put them on now.' He left her holding them and walked over to one of the armchairs near the window. He sat down and waved a mocking invitation towards the mirror. 'Go ahead. Aren't you dying to see them twinkling on your ears?'

'I didn't ask for them, Jared,' she said quietly.

'Wear them,' he commanded, his eyes hard. 'I always intended to give them to my bride...if I ever married.'

A discomfiting sense of guilt wormed through Laura. He had intended these diamonds for a woman he loved. On the other hand, he was not exactly young and he hadn't married so far, although he'd surely had plenty of opportunities over the years. For all she knew, he might not even be capable of loving any woman. He needn't have agreed to marry her. Whether he liked the situation or not, he had chosen to have her as his bride. And he wanted her to put on a show for his mother's benefit.

Laura moved over to the mirror without any further argument. She was chillingly aware of him watching her as she opened the box. The earrings glittered up at her, each a pink diamond centred in a baguette cluster of white diamonds—much smaller than the pendant, of course, but still fabulous. Her hands trembled a little as she removed her gold studs and fastened a large fortune to each earlobe.

'They suit you well enough,' he said sardonically. 'I thought they would.'

'I'm glad you're satisfied,' Laura returned coolly.

His eyes glittered with some dangerously strong emotion for a moment, but he controlled it and nodded towards the bed. 'Is that bit of frivolity a hat?'

'Yes. Would you like to see that on also?'

'Why not?' he drawled.

She was still positioning it on her head when the jeweller returned. Jared answered the door but didn't ask him in again. Laura heard him thank the man. Then he came back to her. 'Very classy,' he commented on the hat, then opened the larger of the two boxes he had carried in and lifted out the pendant.

Laura's skin prickled with sensitivity as he fastened it around her throat. Their eyes met in the mirror and for one brief moment they stared at each other—strangers who were about to enter into the most intimate relationship between a man and a woman.

'Now the ring,' Jared murmured, his face tightening as though that moment had disturbed him in some way.

He slid the ring on her finger. The pink diamond was slightly larger than those in the earrings but the design was exactly the same. Jared immediately collected the boxes and tossed them in her suitcase. 'If there's nothing else to be packed, I'll call the porter,' he said, already moving towards the telephone.

Thirty minutes later Laura was checked out of the hotel and they were in the private lift which serviced Jared's penthouse apartment. The nervous flutter in Laura's stomach had nothing to do with the speedy lift to the top of the building. Jared's tension was affecting her badly. When the lift stopped, he didn't immediately step through the opened doors. He leaned forward and pressed the close-door button, then seemed to gather himself before turning to her.

'Remember that my mother and stepfather mean nothing to you. In normal circumstances you would know nothing of them. Pretend that.'

She nodded, ironically aware of the truth that his mother and stepfather didn't mean anything to her. She didn't even know their names! 'If that's what we're pretending, don't forget to make a formal introduction, Jared.'

His eyes mocked any necessity to be reminded of such a critical detail, but Laura felt better about carrying off her role with that point clearly settled.

'And you can also pretend that you and I, my darling...' his mouth curled over the affectionate term '...are a very happy couple. So smile.'

She smiled.

'Not bad,' he approved, and linked her arm with his in a properly possessive fashion. 'A bit more warmth and sparkle would be more convincing.'

'Give it to me and I'll give it you,' she retorted archly.

She could feel him relax as he gave his low laugh. 'I'll do more than that. One thing you can be certain of... Tonight you'll know what it's like to be my wife. All I have to do is think of that and no one's going to doubt how I feel about you.'

A tidal wave of heat surged through Laura as his eyes blazed down at her with furnace-explosive intent. He was going to reduce her to just another female in one arena of their married life, even if he could never achieve it any other way. It was not so much sexual desire as a blistering need to get the better of her in the age-old way of male domination. And while Laura recognised all this, and part of her mind railed against it, the rest of her was exquisitely excited by the prospect.

A triumphant amusement glittered in his eyes as he observed the high colour in her cheeks. He even smiled as he stroked her burning skin with a light finger-touch. 'You now have the warmth. Don't forget the smile, darling. A little sparkle is required. Think of diamonds,' he purred, then moved his finger to the lift button to reopen the doors.

She would out-glitter him if it killed her, Laura thought, and as they emerged from the small compartment and walked towards the archway which led into the lounge-room she constructed a smile that outshone the Eastern Star. However, she was not prepared for the shock that hit her when they entered the room, and the couple waiting for them rose from the far sofa. It took all of Laura's considerable self-discipline to keep the smile firmly in place.

The face of the woman was older, but its beauty was unchanged...and the haunted eyes were those that looked out of the painting—seeking something...remembering something...aching for something that was forever lost. And they clung to Laura's face as if they were seeing a spectre that filled her soul with torment.

'Laura, this is my mother and stepfather, Naomi and Rafe Carellan,' Jared introduced, and she heard the faint disquiet in his voice even though he tried to project a relaxed indulgence.

Naomi…a soft waft of sound that would echo through the ranges of the Kimberley and whisper across straw-pale plains and linger in the blue shades of twilight…Naomi…and the haunted-haunting eyes kept clinging to Laura's face, bringing a tension to the room that no amount of acting could dispel.

Rafe Carellan jerked his hand out towards Laura in an effort to distract attention from his wife's distraught state of mind, but the hand was clasped tightly by the woman at his side.

'It is…' she whispered hoarsely, then spoke in slow, tortured little bursts. 'You must see it, Rafe. Jared is deceiving us…is deceiving me. They're Drew's eyes. His hairline. It's no wild coincidence. She can't be anyone else. She is Drew's daughter.'

And the past that Jared had wanted to keep in the past was no longer there. It was here…vibrantly alive in this room…and throbbing with pain.

CHAPTER SIX

THE soft beauty of Naomi Carellan's face tightened and twisted in unbearable distress. 'When does the punishment stop?' she cried. Her eyes filled with tears and she turned blindly to her husband for comfort. 'Does it never end, Rafe?'

His arms came around her, gently protective in their embrace. She leaned on him, an instinctive movement that had the familiarity of long practice... years of leaning... of needing and being given support. And the huge, solid frame of the man who gave it stood rock-steady. But his face was also creased in suffering. Whether it was compassion for his wife or a deep personal pain of his own, it was impossible to tell.

He was almost an ugly man. His heavy-featured face was set on a bull-neck, and his deeply freckled skin suggested that the wispy white hair had once been red. But the soft brown eyes had an intensely human appeal that contrasted sharply with the toughness of his exterior.

'What's going on, Jared?' he demanded quietly.

'How can Mother be so certain?' Jared bit out tightly.

'The name. The place. Drew told her about his first marriage. The daughter he'd given up so she could have a full-time father. And what *that* cost him in personal agony as well. It weighed heavily on his mind. His child... the daughter he would never have... and wanted. He talked a lot about her...'

Her father had wanted her... loved her, Laura thought dazedly. She hadn't been wrong about him. He had done what he thought best for her. At great cost to himself...

'I hoped it was just a coincidence,' Rafe continued. 'That she would be a different Laura Hammond from Boston...' His grimace was savagely rueful. 'Too much to hope for. But that's no reason for you to sacrifice yourself for the sins of the past, Jared.'

It was a struggle for Laura to break out of the shock that had held her mind and body rigid for the last few minutes. The trauma that her identity had triggered had been so unexpected...so appalling...and the realisation that this was what Jared had wanted to avoid...that he thought she had known that her father's painting—the past—could have this terrible effect...

She had to stop it, mitigate it, repair the damage she had so blithely and unwittingly done in her ignorance. Before Jared could say anything—say the wrong thing—she rushed into speech.

'Mr Carellan, I'm not what your wife thinks...' She pushed her feet forward and reached out to the woman who was still weeping on her husband's broad shoulder. She gently squeezed her arm. 'Please don't cry. Jared didn't want to upset you. And neither did I. I can't help being my father's daughter, any more than Jared can help being your son. And both of us want to let the past go. Please don't let it hurt you...like this...'

The tear-ravaged face turned slowly towards Laura, deep blue eyes awash with painful uncertainty. 'Why...why are you marrying my son?'

'I couldn't help falling in love with him,' Laura answered without a second's hesitation, instinctively knowing it was the only answer that could allay Naomi Carellan's fears. She smiled a soft reassurance. 'I'm sorry. But I do love him. And he loves me.'

'Jared?' Naomi Carellan shook her head in pained incredulity, then turned to stare accusingly at her son. 'How could you?'

Jared's face was unrelievedly grim. Laura's heart sank at the prospect of having her words denied, and the truth of their marriage arrangement laid bare. This was the critical moment—to go forward or retreat—and Laura fiercely willed Jared to back her up. To go on in the face of what had just happened was madness, of course. It was the result of making too many decisions without enough information. But now that they had reached this point, Laura didn't want the arrangement they had made cast aside. She knew there was no going back for her. Come hell or high water, she was going to marry Jared Eastern. If she could.

She sought desperately for something else to say, but it was up to him...if he wanted the deception to continue...if he wanted the marriage to go on. She realised she couldn't make it happen without his co-operation.

'Laura can hardly be blamed for what happened, Mother,' he reproved tersely, but his eyes were glinting daggers of fire, suggestive of a raging blaze of thoughts that were not being expressed...as yet. There was no commitment in those words, nothing to indicate which way he would move.

He stepped forward and put his arm around Laura, hugging her close to him in a show of protective support. 'I didn't plan to fall in love with her,' he said, and Laura was intensely grateful she could lean on his strength, because her legs seemed to have turned to water. He was going on with it, her mind sang, then swiftly settled to an acute state of alertness in order to keep up her end of the deception.

'And I didn't know who she was until we'd been meeting for some time,' Jared continued. 'The name of Hammond meant nothing to me.'

'I didn't know who Jared was at first either,' Laura put in quickly. 'It sounds incredible, but we were just strangers, and we looked at each other across a room full of people...'

'And the attraction was instant...spontaneous... and irrevocable,' Jared declared with such ringing conviction that even Laura would have believed him, if she hadn't known better. 'Look at Laura, Mother!' he commanded. 'Don't see her as Drew's daughter. See her for the beautiful woman she is...the woman I've been waiting for all my life...the woman who'll make me the wife I need...'

He dug his fingers into her arm and Laura glanced up at him on cue, flashing a quick smile to meet the adoring look he was pouring down at her. What could pass as an adoring look, anyway. It held a burning intensity that made Laura's heart catch and flutter. For the first time ever she saw Jared's mouth soften into what could be called a lovingly indulgent smile. Then he turned his gaze back to his mother and delivered another eloquent plea.

'What happened between you and Drew and my father has nothing to do with us, Mother. It's in the past. Laura and I want the future. Together. If that's hard to accept, I'm sorry. But that's the way it's going to be.'

The beautiful face looked more haunted than ever, distraught with memories that Laura had no way of knowing. Her father...Naomi...Jared's father...the age-old triangle perhaps? And what had happened to Jared's father? But she couldn't think of that now. The compelling need to set the past aside drove her to support Jared's act with every emotional force she could muster. Her hand gestured an appeal for understanding.

'We hoped you could be happy for us if you didn't know who I was,' she explained. 'It seemed...a harmless deception. I'm sorry you've been so deeply distressed by it. We wanted...we thought...' Her eyes lifted imploringly to Rafe Carellan's sympathetic gaze. 'Is it so wrong for Jared and I to get married?'

'No,' he answered firmly. 'Maybe it will be the one thing that sets everything right. It's good. Incredible in a way. Even if someone tried to arrange it, one would hardly dare to hope...' He heaved a satisfied sigh and nodded approvingly as he added, 'That it should happen naturally is good!'

'Rafe...' Naomi reproached hoarsely. 'The stakes are too high. If Jared is made to suffer...'

Rafe Carellan's eyes raked over Laura. 'Jared won't suffer. And it's always been on my conscience that I let Drew walk away. For all that I told myself it was his choice to make, I should have made him take...what he had every right to take.'

So Rafe had been part of it too. Three men...and a beautiful woman...and a boy...and a diamond mine. But Laura couldn't afford to think about it. Not at this moment. Later. For the present only Jared really counted. She had to keep him at her side...keep alert to do or say whatever was required.

Rafe Carellan drew in a deep breath then turned his wife around to face him, his hands gently caressing her arms as his eyes begged her to listen. 'Naomi...we've come so far. Both of us. Let it go now...let it go. This is another time...another generation. Don't visit the sins of the parents upon the children.'

'Oh God, Rafe!' It was a broken cry of despair. 'What would I do without you?'

His arms enclosed her gently against his heart. 'You'll never have to do without me, Naomi. Not as long as God lets me live.' He rubbed his cheek over her hair in soothing reassurance, but his eyes were on Laura, urgently questioning.

She didn't know how she knew what he was asking. But the answer slipped off her tongue without any deep consideration. 'My father died last year. His heart gave out. It's over... for him.'

Rafe's relief was almost a tangible thing, yet there was an apology in his eyes for it. 'There was no way to fix it, Laura,' he said quietly. 'He must have told you that. If there was, we would have done it.'

Her father hadn't told her anything, but she believed Rafe Carellan. He emitted an air of integrity that was impossible to doubt. Whatever had happened all those years ago had been a tragedy that had affected more than her father's life. If there had been some injustice done to him, no one had profited from it. Not in the terms that really counted. Not even a mountain full of diamonds could make up for this kind of human misery.

'Drew became a highly regarded artist in his latter years,' Jared stated, injecting a note of matter-of-fact calmness into the overfraught atmosphere. 'Some of his paintings are hanging in the New South Wales Art Gallery. He signed them Andy Mac. Perhaps, Mother, you would like to go and see them.'

And Laura knew then why *the* painting had had to come off the wall. If Naomi Carellan had walked into the art gallery and seen her portrait... Laura shuddered.

'I'm glad he found another way to be successful,' Rafe said, and it was clear that another burden had lifted from his mind. 'Did you hear that, Naomi?'

He eased her slightly away from him and cupped her face with his hands, gently forcing her to meet his eyes. 'Drew's life wasn't ruined. And we're not going to ruin Jared's and Laura's. We're going to wish them every happiness there can be between a man and a woman. And tomorrow we will go out and look at Drew's paintings. That will make you happy, won't it?'

The gentle consideration in Rafe Carellan's speech shook Laura. It was almost the benevolent action of a parent talking to soothe a child's worst fears. It vividly recalled to mind the lost quality that her father had painted into the portrait.

'Yes,' came the husky reply. Her fragile shoulders lifted and fell as she gulped in a steadying breath. Then she turned around to face Laura and Jared. 'I'm sorry...' Her lips quivered and she bit them, her eyes anxiously pleading forgiveness.

Laura stepped forward and took her hands with her own, pressing them warmly. 'It was the shock. It does that to people. You don't have to apologise, Mrs Carellan. Please...let's all sit down and...' She shot a questioning look at Jared. 'I'm sure you have a bottle of champagne somewhere, haven't you, darling?'

He gave her a cold, hard, probing look. 'I surely do. Champagne coming up.'

It was a stiff, awkward conversation to begin with, even with the champagne that Jared plied with relentless persuasion. Rafe did his best to ease the tension, asking Laura about her life in Boston. She skated over that very quickly and led on to the more neutral ground of her travels in other countries.

'Do you think you'll be happy, living at Bendeneer Downs?'

Laura was so used now to answering questions relating to things that were completely beyond her comprehension that she had no difficulty at all with this one. She didn't have the foggiest notion where Bendeneer Downs was, or what it was, but she took it in her stride.

'I've lived happily in England. And I've lived happily in France——'

'What Laura is saying...or trying to say,' Jared cut in, 'is that she will be happy living anywhere.'

'Thank you.' She beamed him a loving smile.

'I can't say I was.' It was Naomi's first effort to enter the conversation and the statement carried a tight edge of concern.

Rafe took her hand and patted it reassuringly. 'My dear, some people suit one environment. Others need different places. Your place is in the city.'

She shook her head. 'I never liked it. It's men's country. No place for a woman...' her eyes seemed to lose their focus and her voice dropped to a whisper as she added '...and dreadful things happen.'

'It won't happen this time around,' Jared declared decisively.

Naomi's deep blue eyes fastened anxiously, almost feverishly on Laura. 'If you have any difficulty, you can always come to me. Don't wait too long. Don't let it eat into you. Get away before...before——'

'Naomi...' Rafe squeezed her hand hard, drawing her attention back to him. 'It's different now from what it was. Bendeneer Downs has every civilised comfort. Every facility. And with a helicopter on hand, it's not so isolated any more. Besides, Jared can afford to look after Laura's happiness. Stop worrying, my dear.'

She gave a little shudder and subsided into passive silence again.

Bendeneer Downs must be some kind of settlement near the diamond mine, Laura figured. Probably where the miners now lived. Men's country. But she had been to the Kimberley and been fascinated by that strange ancient land. She could live there. She could live anywhere. Jared probably didn't know how true that was when he had spoken those words.

Oddly enough, after his mother's strained little speech, Jared seemed to withdraw into himself. Although he continued to contribute to the conversation, it was as if he had put one part of his mind on automatic drive to deal with that. His more intense concentration was definitely channelled on to something else. Laura sensed a growing tension in him that started to play havoc with her nerves as the zero-hour of their marriage approached.

There was still time for him to change his mind about going through with it. Was he reconsidering? His mother's fears had been soothed. The worst of any trauma was over. Maybe he thought he would now be paying too much, since one of his motives for agreeing to the marriage had been cleared away.

Laura breathed a very shaky sigh of relief when the hour finally came and a party of men arrived at the apartment: Jared's solicitor, a photographer, the marriage celebrant, and two witnesses who turned out to be executives in Jared's company. Introductions were made and glasses of champagne offered around.

They were on their feet, virtually at the altar in a manner of speaking. And then, precisely when Laura was beginning to think she was safe, that the marriage was definitely on, Jared tucked her arm around his, holding it there with very purposeful determination, and announced to the group at large, 'Please excuse us for a few minutes. Laura and I have a few private things to do. We'll be right back.'

He gave Laura no choice in the matter. He had her arm in a vice-like grip, and, short of undoing the impression of loving harmony that had carried them this far, she had to pretend this was what she wanted too. But it wasn't. It struck panic into her heart. She didn't know what she was going to do if Jared meant to back out now.

He steered her into a bedroom and closed the door behind them with an air of grim purpose. He released her arm, but he lifted his hands and held her shoulders to ensure her facing him as he said what he'd planned to say.

Laura's entire nervous system was in chaos. Nevertheless, desperation put a fine edge on her mind, and she was determined on fighting for what she wanted if Jared gave her any leeway at all. Somehow she kept her eyes calm and unwavering as he frowned down at her, the green eyes sharply intent and probing hard.

'Firstly, I want to thank you for the way you handled the situation with my mother and Rafe. It was done with finesse and compassion. Whatever else you are, I have to salute you for that.'

Impossible to tell him she would never deliberately set out to hurt anyone. Putting the painting in the exhibition damned her on that score. There was only one reply to make if she was to keep their arrangement in place.

'I did what we agreed upon, Jared,' she reminded him flatly. 'You asked me to pretend I was madly in love with you. I did and said whatever was consistent with that role. And, having established it, I'll keep it going whenever we're in the presence of your family.' She constructed an ironic little smile. 'It's a matter of integrity.'

His frown cut deeper. Then with a sharp, negative jerk of his head, he released her and turned away, walking across the room to a huge window which looked out over the city. He stood there for several moments, but Laura didn't imagine he was considering the view. His back was stiff with tension.

'For whatever reason...you did something that no one else has been able to do. And I no longer feel justified in going on with what I meant to do,' he said with terse finality.

Defeat hammered through her heart even while her mind sought frantically for an argument that might persuade him to reconsider. 'So...you're welshing on the agreement,' she threw at him acidly.

He swung around, his mouth a sardonic twist, his eyes agleam with self-mockery. 'No, I'm letting *you* off the hook. I'll write you an open cheque. Anything you like. You can walk away from this with all your heart's desire. No pain at all.'

'And what if I don't want to walk away?' she challenged, her head defiantly high as she walked towards him.

His face tightened. 'I've just told you you can write your own ticket. What more can I offer you?'

She stopped, barely a half-pace away from him, and, remembering what he had done to her the previous night, she lifted her hand and lightly stroked her fingers down his cheek. The slight flinch of a muscle under her feathering touch sent a thrill of power through her veins and she smiled into his fierce green eyes, gripped by a heady recklessness that dictated this one last gambit.

'I want you, Jared,' she said softly. 'I won't accept anything else. Not money. Not diamonds. Nor any other terms you can think of. Only you.'

His hand shot up and closed around her wrist, forcing her hand away. 'You won't win that way,' he grated.

'You don't understand.' Her lips quivered a little at the audacity of what she was doing, but she couldn't retreat now. 'I have nothing to lose,' she said, stating the simple truth, although he would never believe it.

'Laura...' His voice was hoarse. He swallowed. 'I warn you. Give it up now. Take your profit and go.'

'No.' Again her eyes coolly challenged him. 'I'll go if you wish, but I'll take nothing with me.'

His fingers almost crushed the bones in her wrist and his eyes blazed with something akin to hatred. 'You'll never do to me what my mother did to your father. I'll never let a woman influence or change my life. Beauty is nothing. A body is just a body. I won't ever fight for you. I certainly won't die for you! And I won't cosset you like a child either! You will only ever be a convenience to me. Do you understand that?' he bit out venomously.

'Yes!' she said, and she did. He had only been a boy, but the trauma of the past had bitten deeply into him too. It was becoming clearer all the time. He blamed it all on his mother's beauty. And maybe his mother had traded on her looks—impossible for Laura to know—but she herself would never trade on such a superficiality. She had never needed a man to fight for her or cosset her or die for her. She simply needed Jared.

Maybe it wouldn't last long. Maybe their differences would be hopelessly irreconcilable and the marriage would prove to be a terrible mistake—as her mother had warned. But until she knew that for certain nothing was going to stop her from having him. Except Jared himself.

'Fine!' he said with an aggressive lift of his chin. And the glitter in his eyes was not wholly hostile. Laura fancied she saw a gleam of relish for the challenge she had thrown him and taken up in return. 'Then let's get married,' he added with a sharp edge of derision.

And without another word or pause, he tucked her arm around his again, marched her straight out to the waiting marriage celebrant, and commanded that the ceremony be performed without another moment's delay.

CHAPTER SEVEN

'WILL YOU, Laura Mary Hammond, take this man...?'

As Laura listened to the words that the marriage celebrant was reciting, her nerve faltered. What manner of man was she taking as her husband? She barely knew him. The reckless certainty that had carried her to this moment wavered. She looked up at Jared Eastern, a sharp question in her eyes. His response to the unguarded flash of vulnerability was an unmistakable gleam of sardonic amusement. It served to put steel into Laura's backbone. Her head snapped back to the celebrant and she stared at him with fixed resolve as he came to the end of the question.

'I will!' she said softly, but firmly enough to deny any doubts whatsoever.

She had done it now, she thought wildly. For better or for worse she had gone through with it. And if she had the devil by the tail, then heaven help her! But never would she show the slightest hint of weakness to Jared Eastern ever again.

He made his responses and signed the papers with total sang-froid. He exuded the air of a person on a victory to nothing, as if certain within himself that he couldn't lose from this situation. Triumph glittered in his eyes as he posed for the photographs. His manner throughout the celebratory drinks that followed was that of a man who had won the prize of a lifetime.

Laura wasn't quite sure if she was excited or frightened at the prospect of being left alone with her newly acquired husband. What he was thinking or feeling, she had no idea. It was impossible to tell if he was still acting or not. Did he figure she had now played into his hands and he could do whatever he wanted with her? Or was he hiding a furious resentment at feeling trapped into marrying her because she wouldn't accept anything else?

But she had given him a choice, Laura reasoned, desperately needing to justify what she had done. Was it her fault that he couldn't believe she would walk away with nothing? Either the sense of debt to her father ran very deep or—underneath all the talk of other considerations—she stirred something in Jared that he didn't want to walk away from any more than she did.

Laura wanted to believe that. She did in her heart of hearts. She couldn't have married him otherwise. But how the next part of the charade would be played was critical to their future relationship. First impressions were strongest, and Laura was quite certain that the coming hours of this day would form impressions that could last all their lives. Her nerves were in a state of fine tension as she and Jared saw Rafe and Naomi into the lift.

They were the last to leave, and for their benefit Jared had his arm around Laura's waist, preserving the image of a devoted bridegroom right up to the second that the steel doors snapped shut, closing off the need for any further pretence.

His fingers tightened their grasp on the soft roundness of her hip and Laura's heart leapt into her throat. She needed him to take her in his arms and kiss her senseless, to smash, crush, and utterly demolish any doubts about the decision she had made. Yet even as she lifted her gaze to his, fiercely hoping to see the desire that answered what she felt, his hand was plucked away, and his eyes met hers with a look of bleak derision.

'The show is almost over,' he drawled. 'Act Two complete. I must offer my congratulations for your superb performance. Excellent. Really excellent. But I wouldn't like you to be counting your success too soon.'

He turned back into the lounge-room, pointedly separating himself from her. He made straight for the table, opened another bottle of Veuve Clicquot and started filling a glass with purposeful deliberation.

Laura did not follow him. She stood in the archway, watching him and fighting the sinking sensation in her stomach. He had been acting. He hated her for what she had done. Or hated the sense of being forced into a corner that was not of his choosing.

She remembered the look he had given her in the lift before she had met Rafe and Naomi—the blazing need to dominate, to reduce her to something that could never again threaten his world. A flash of insight told her that, the more Jared wanted her, the more he would deny it to prove that he was in control.

She had to break that control if they were to ever have the relationship she wanted. And he had let slip that he found her coolness extremely provocative. Now, more than at any other time in her life, she had to be strong. She would not—could not—accept his terms, or she would be nothing to him.

He offered the glass of champagne to her with mocking courtesy. 'Some liquid fortitude? Act Three may not bring out the best in you. Perhaps you would prefer to be dead drunk.'

Every instinct, every intuitive power she had, told her unequivocally that this was the critical moment of decision. If she didn't handle this situation correctly, he would never respect her again. His kind of strength only respected strength.

He did not see what was coming. Had no way of anticipating it. Laura carefully controlled all expression on her face. The grey eyes mirrored nothing of her inner churning. The clear serenity that frustrated her mother so much was a well-practised mask that could not be pierced. She walked towards him with a slow, deliberate grace that projected absolute confidence.

It held his attention. His eyes were wary. His body had the stillness of a wild animal whose every sense was alert, suspicious and untrusting. He waited for the end-play of her move. When she halted her approach to him a half-arm's length away, but did not take the glass offered, he waited for her to speak.

Laura did not hit him with the full force of her body. The open-handed slap was controlled. It was meant to sting, not to hurt. To mark without wounding. And to assert her dignity.

'Never speak to me like that again!' she commanded frostily. 'I'm your equal, Jared Eastern. I've just become your partner. And you're going to treat me that way. Because I won't accept anything else.'

He did not move. The dangerous flare in his eyes was neutralised. Laura could feel the intense concentration of his mind as he harnessed every ounce of control to his purpose. His lips twisted into a half-semblance of a smile.

'Very refined!' he drawled. 'So refined and civilised one might almost think that you reflected true Bostonian culture. But that's only a veneer, isn't it, Laura? And beneath the veneer is a savage who wants blood. But let me tell you here and now—you won't draw it from me.'

'Perhaps it's not blood that I'm after, Jared,' she retorted mockingly. 'Perhaps it's something else entirely. But I doubt you'll ever find out.'

He drank the glass of champagne in virtually one gulp, then hurled the glass across the floor. The switch from control to violence was so fast that it caught Laura unprepared, and before she could make any evasive or protective move he had her crushed against him, his arms as unrelenting as hoops of steel.

'God damn you!' he seethed, and the savagery in his eyes was glaring evidence that the wild animal was slipping its civilised leash. 'I've had enough! You've taken my patience to the limit. You've cost me personally far too much. And you're not getting away with this. I'll break you if I have to, so you'd better start bending, Laura...'

His chest heaved as he drew breath and Laura didn't need to be psychic to sense the turbulent violence that was on the edge of explosion. Fight or flight were out. To oppose him was totally dangerous, with consequences completely unforeseeable...and results she might not want.

'Now kiss me, you computerised little hell-cat!' he hissed in fierce demand. 'Kiss me...because I'm going to kiss you. I'm going to kiss you until I find out what you really are. And then I'm going to take you...take you to places you've never been with any man before. Then after that we'll see how quickly you rush into your filthy little sordid divorce schemes.'

Laura barely had time to register the blistering accusation. No chance to speak. As his lips came down to take possession of her own, she did the only thing possible. For the moment, she surrendered.

There was no attempt to woo a response with sensuality this time. No intention to explore or seduce. His kiss was a blitzkrieg, an invasion so sudden and violently aggressive that no defence could have been mounted, let alone maintained. His mouth stormed hers, ravished it, eclipsing all thought with sensations that powered through her entire body, setting off a surge of adrenalin that demanded an instant end to any submissiveness.

Something deep and savagely primitive stirred inside Laura and clawed with the need to reach into him, to stun and invade and take and possess, to wreak as intensive a violation on him as he was wreaking on her. She met his second kiss with a kamikaze passion that recognised only one target, and the ultimate cost to herself was totally irrelevant.

It excited him into relaxing the imprisoning embrace, his hands moving to pressure her lower body into meeting the desire that had leapt beyond his control. Laura lifted her arms, wound them around his neck, and arched her body against his with all the wanton provocation of her feminine sexuality. A low growl issued, feeding on what she gave and took, greedy for each wild foray of passion that fought for a domination which neither would concede.

The hat was plucked from her head and thrown away, hairpins drawn and dropped, the thick coil of her hair raked into disarray. Strong fingers thrust through the silky mane, curled around her skull, and wrenched her head back from his.

A low, exultant laugh gravelled from Jared's throat and Laura stared up at him with glazed eyes, frantically ordering her mind to lift above the chaos of sensation which plundered it of any ability to reason. His gaze glittered over the long, straight tresses of her hair.

'Yes...' he hissed. 'That's your true colour. Black! Witch-black! And a pagan heart to match. So let's get rid of all the deceptive trappings.'

Jared dragged and tore the clothes from her body, but the madness of his violent impatience to have her naked stirred an equally aggressive pride which insisted that she offer no resistance. There was no sense of humiliation, only a bubbling exultation that she had goaded him so far. He was breathing hard when he completed the frenzied despoiling of her outer finery and he looked at her, standing still and tall and proud before him, her only adornment the diamonds he had given her, and a fierce satisfaction lit his eyes.

'Like some pagan queen from the past,' he said, and with a wilder laugh than before he scooped her up in his arms and marched off to the bedroom like a conqueror of old carrying off the spoils of victory.

He spilled her on to the bed, but with a graceful roll of her body Laura managed to finish up in a challenging position on her back, her gaze meeting his with taunting directness. Her heart was pounding at an unbelievable rate. Every sense she had was alive with excitement. There was no sanity in anything that was happening. She was acting on pure instinct. This was a contest of power, the most primitive power of all—man against woman . . . woman against man—and, if he was going to take her to places she had never been before with any other man, she was going to take him to where he had never been with any other woman!

'Witch!' he threw at her, his eyes glittering an acknowledgement of the battle she silently promised him as he stripped off his clothes.

He was beautifully made, sleekly muscled, firmly fleshed, his body honed to strength and power, his skin bronzed to a smooth polish that made Laura ache to touch him. There was a fever in her blood she had never known before, a high pitch of awareness that sang through her body, wanting a satiation of every sense until there was nothing more to be experienced.

She couldn't help smiling as he knelt over her. It wasn't meant to inflame him. It was simply an involuntary expression of glorious anticipation. But it sparked an explosive reaction from Jared. 'No!' he rasped, and snatched up her hands, slamming them above her head as he lowered his formidable weight on to her pliant softness, his eyes watching, gloating with the superiority of his male strength. 'You won't have your way with me. And you won't be smiling when I've finished with you,' he promised grimly.

'Won't I?' She writhed her hips in deliberate incitement, loving the feel of his nakedness against hers... the vibrant power of his masculinity, the sensual heat of his skin, the silky roughness of hair that raised an electric sensitivity. 'Kiss me, Jared,' she invited huskily. 'Kiss the smile off my lips.'

If there had been any thread of sanity left before that wanton moment of provocation, there was none after it. Not one vestige of control from either of them. Any thought of contest was forgotten in a mindless need to capture all that there could be between them; to tear the breath from each other, to touch and taste and exult in sensation after sensation... exquisite, erotic, voluptuous pleasure-pain that kept building and building, fuelling the explosive desire to possess all they could of each other to the most intimate depths—past every barrier, into the unknown, and beyond it to whatever came after.

The sheer rapture of the ultimate merging of their bodies was so intense that even Jared paused to catch his breath. Their eyes met, clung, and some wordless indefinable acknowledgement was made, a pure moment of recognition that was reinforced again and again as he went on, driving himself to plunge deeper and faster to the very centre of her being as she contracted and melted around him, fire to fire, force meeting force, man and woman in the age-old rhythm of mating, body to body, soul to soul, to the final melding that made it complete.

They lay together afterwards, entwined in an embrace that neither made any move to break. No word was spoken. Neither made any concession to the other. But the silence they kept held a sense of peace, as if a treaty had been signed and ratified. And there would be no more fighting. Not over this. In this, if in nothing else, they were equals... partners... at one with each other. They were both winners.

Whether Jared could remain satisfied with that or not Laura couldn't tell, but she was content that he showed no inclination to part from her. What she had just experienced with him was what she had always wanted, although she had never been able to define it before. Couldn't define it even now.

She didn't fool herself that everything would be perfect between her and Jared from this moment on. There were far too many hurdles to cross before any mutual understanding could be reached ... if it ever was. She couldn't even say that she loved him, although she loved what he had made her feel with him. They were right for each other, in a way that transcended all other differences, but it still might not be enough to forge the kind of marriage that Laura would be happy with.

But she had been right to go through with it. She might never have known this ... ever ... with anyone else. And when she drifted into sleep a smile was on her lips ... not wiped off as Jared had initially intended. It was a smile of knowledge that could never be taken away from her.

CHAPTER EIGHT

THE feather-light stroke on Laura's cheek raised her consciousness and the soft call of her name brought her instantly awake. Morning light flooded the room and Jared was sitting on the bed beside her, his hair dark with dampness, his jaw shiny from having been shaved, the tangy scent of some male toiletry accentuating his smell of fresh cleanliness.

'You wake like a cat. Instantly alert,' he said in sardonic appreciation. 'I've let you sleep as late as possible but time is moving on, and we have a flight to make, remember? I'm sure you don't want to miss out on seeing all the possessions you've acquired by marrying me.'

She didn't like the hard, mocking glint in his eyes. She wondered, for a moment, if last night had been a dream, and then she recollected his blistering words about her divorce schemes. She didn't want him thinking like that, but it was clear he would mistrust any straightforward denial from her. If she couldn't win him over, maybe it would come to divorce in the end anyway. The thought of defeat was surprisingly painful.

Instinctively she reached out to him, wanting to recapture the togetherness they had known in the heat of lovemaking. 'I don't expect they're possessions that will disappear if I don't see them straight away, Jared,' she suggested softly, moving her hand over his bare chest in an inviting caress.

He caught her wrist, his fingers almost crushing the bones as he halted any further movement. His jaw went rigid with determination and the green eyes flared with a violence of feeling that swiftly crystallised into inflexible purpose.

'No one runs my life, Laura. Least of all a woman,' he stated grimly. 'Legally you are now my partner. You may even be my equal. As my wife, you can come with me if you wish. Or go your own way. But I'm leaving here in an hour and I don't intend to be delayed. What you choose to do is your own affair.'

Partner...equal...the words were sweet to Laura's ears. Progress had been made with him! 'You're hurting my wrist, Jared,' she said, secretly satisfied that her touch had a very definite effect on him also.

His eyes mockingly reminded her that the power to arouse was not one-sided as he lifted her wrist to his lips and kissed the pulse-point with a slow sensuality which immediately accelerated her heartbeat. 'Better now?' he asked sardonically.

'Improving.'

He laughed and released her, standing up in an abrupt dismissal of any further physical intimacy. 'Breakfast in half an hour if you're coming with me,' he tossed over his shoulder as he strode towards the dressing-room.

The towel knotted around his lean hips was a frustrating interruption to Laura's view of him, but the rippling muscles of his back and the lithe power of his legs ignited memories that had her stretching with languorous pleasure. Tonight, she thought, and tomorrow night and...

'I'll be ready,' she said, pushing herself out of bed.

He paused in the doorway to look back at her, his eyes flicking over her nakedness before he answered with dry cynicism, 'Somehow I knew you'd want to come back to Bendeneer with me, Laura.'

She laughed, unable to contain the delicious sense of anticipation that bubbled through her. 'It suits my purpose, Jared.'

'Undoubtedly.' His mouth twisted. 'It will be interesting to see how long it continues to suit your purpose.'

'Perhaps "until death us do part". Have you considered that, Jared?' she retorted lightly, hoping it might shift his thoughts off divorce.

His reaction was chilling. His face darkened. His eyes iced over. 'If you want it all to yourself, Laura, you'll wait a long time,' he bit out contemptuously. 'I won't die as easily as my father did. And you'd never get away with another killing between our families. Rafe would see to that.'

Numb with shock, Laura had no control whatsoever over the horrified question that fell from her lips. 'Who killed whom?'

'I suppose your father called it an accident,' he said bitterly. 'It's wonderful how people can twist things around. Although it's true enough he was attacked first. But it was my father who ended up dead. Don't overlook that in your nice, neat calculations. I don't. And I won't.'

Laura shook her head, too dazed by the ghastly revelation to argue that she had no calculations at all. And it was like a stab in the heart that Jared could think she would be so base as to consider his death as a means of gain. She took a deep breath to settle the nausea billowing through her stomach. Whatever had happened in the past had nothing to do with her, she reasoned fiercely. She had married Jared Eastern and she was going to keep him, come what may.

Her chin lifted in defiant challenge. 'The trouble with you, Jared, is you're not used to women who can't be bought off. But it's nice to know I'm a new experience for you.'

His eyes narrowed as she walked towards him with all the confidence that last night had given her. She paused beside him, reached up and stroked her fingers down his cheek in deliberate provocation. 'And please don't waste your time worrying about your skin on my account, Jared. Because I want you alive. Very much alive.' Then she passed by him, through the dressing-room to the en-suite bathroom.

Laura felt his eyes boring into her every step of the way and marvelled at her own temerity. She shut the door behind her with a sense of triumphant satisfaction. She had given him something positive to think about. And he wanted her. She had seen the unquenchable flare of desire in his eyes as she had moved away. There was something explosive between them that he couldn't deny any more than she could. And, while they had that together, they had a future!

She caught sight of her reflection in the mirror above the vanity-bench and realised she still wore the diamonds he had given her. The diamonds for his wife! And she wasn't about to give up that position in a hurry!

Let the past go—that was what they had agreed on yesterday. So let it be, she thought fiercely. There was more to his father's death than Jared was saying, or Rafe's and Naomi's reactions yesterday would have been different. And even if her father was guilty of some grievous wrong, he had paid for it, leading the life of a lonely outcast. But that was no longer her main concern. And she wasn't going to let it interfere with her chance of happiness.

Happiness? she questioned, staring at herself in the mirror with eyes that suddenly seemed brighter than ever before. Could this wild madness with Jared be called happiness? An endless pitting of strength against strength, a duel of wits spiced by the strong attraction they felt for each other, a fight to the finish . . . and what was the finish she wanted?

For Jared to love her . . . to need her . . . to want her in his life forever . . .

The thoughts rolled through her mind and clung with overwhelming force. Her heart kicked over in a funny little leap. She shook her head, amazed at how simple it all was. *He* was the man for her! It didn't matter why she should feel that. *He* was the one!

Except it wasn't simple at all where Jared was concerned. She was in for a fight all right! But at least she knew her own mind . . . knew precisely where she was going. How to get there was the problem! But she *was* his wife. That was an advantage no other woman had ever had.

Laura was late for breakfast. Jared was already seated at the dining table, applying himself to a plate of bacon and eggs and reading a newspaper which was propped beside it. Definitely not waiting for her.

'I can't find the clothes you tore off me last night,' she announced brightly.

It drew his attention. 'I imagine Evelyn will have taken care of them,' he replied, his eyes flicking over the T-shirt and jeans Laura had chosen to wear. The glossy mass of her black hair was clipped back at the nape of her neck in her usual style. Her face was devoid of make-up, but her skin glowed and her eyes danced back at him. His mouth twitched in sardonic amusement. 'Quite a change of image! Another little surprise for me?'

She grinned at him. 'No. Just my usual travelling gear. If it's not appropriate, tell me so.' He was in casual clothes himself so she expected no criticism. The green sports shirt accentuated the colour of his eyes and Laura thought he was certainly the most striking man she had ever met. 'And who's Evelyn?' she added, since he seemed preoccupied with other thoughts.

'Evelyn Geary,' he replied offhandedly. 'She takes care of everything in this apartment. If you step into the kitchen and introduce yourself she will answer all your needs. Including breakfast. Tell her what you want.'

Evelyn Geary was a homely middle-aged woman who seemed genuinely pleased to meet Jared Eastern's new wife. Laura's clothes had been set aside for cleaning. Laura's breakfast was promptly cooked and served. Jared watched her eat it with an air of impatience.

'When you're ready,' he grated as she blithely poured herself a second cup of coffee. His ultimatum of an hour had slipped by ten minutes previously.

Laura looked up, all innocent co-operation. 'I'm ready. I needn't have had breakfast. You suggested it, Jared.'

He sliced her a mocking look as he stood up. 'Oddly enough, I want you alive too, Laura.' He rounded the table and held out her chair for her. 'After all, it's not every day one acquires a wife...' his fingers brushed her cheek as she rose to her feet '...with so many fine qualities.'

She laughed out of sheer exhilaration. Not only had she delayed him when he had sworn no woman would ever do that, but he was an opponent of skilful finesse and she enjoyed the thrust and parry of their complex relationship.

She was in high spirits as they left the apartment and travelled to the airport where the Lear Jet was ready waiting for them. Jared introduced her to the pilot and a steward who was employed to look after any refreshments they required. The aeroplane was fitted out with every possible comfort: sitting-room, bedroom, bathroom, and a very sophisticated galley to prepare meals. Laura was really looking forward to seeing the diamond mine and learning all about Jared's life, and she strapped herself into an armchair for take-off in a mood of happy anticipation. She looked across at Jared, who was eyeing her with somewhat bemused speculation.

'You never did tell me why we have to fly to Bendeneer today,' she remarked questioningly.

'I don't like missing a muster.'

'I thought you dug diamonds out of the ground. I didn't know you could muster them.' She didn't know much about mining at all and that term certainly didn't fit her limited knowledge.

His mouth quirked. 'Not diamonds. Cattle. Diamond mining is my work. Running one of the largest cattle stations in the world is my pleasure. Particularly at this time.'

Laura hid her confusion as best she could. They were flying to the mine ... but he was going to muster cattle? 'You never mentioned this before,' she said, hoping it would prompt him into expanding the contradictory information.

'Then there was something you didn't know!' The green eyes danced with cynical amusement. 'The mine runs itself, Laura. As you must know from visiting it. The loading, crushing, conveying and cleaning are all computer-controlled. At a pinch, the whole plant could be run by six people. There is no challenge in that. The diamond-cutting is done in Perth, and Rafe takes care of everything there. I need to do things. To achieve things. So I look after the international side of the diamond marketing with De Beers. But my real life is Bendeneer Downs. That's where I spend most of my time. And I wouldn't give up that life for anything or anyone. I like the challenge. I like the response. I like controlling the uncontrollable.'

The information finally gelled in Laura's mind. Bendeneer Downs had nothing to do with the diamond mine! It was a cattle station! One of the vast open-range properties in the Kimberley ... self-sufficient, isolated, frontier country, with hundreds of miles between neighbours. She suddenly understood what Naomi had been talking about yesterday. Men's country... no place for a woman...

Jared was watching her... watching the realisation sink in. 'It's a mistress that no woman could ever match,' he said with goading certainty. 'People come and go, but the land is there forever; endlessly testing, demanding, driving a man to the limits of his capabilities and endurance; giving rewards and punishments that exalt and crush.' His eyes gleamed with mockery as he added, 'But I can hardly expect a lady from Boston to understand that.'

She smiled. 'You really shouldn't make a habit of underestimating me, Jared. It's a long time since I've lived in Boston. Even there I learnt to live in an alien environment.'

'Alien?' The mockery was replaced by a spark of curiosity.

'Maybe one day I'll tell you about it. Now is not the time.'

Cynicism curled his mouth. 'You prefer to intrigue me.'

'Let's just say that endurance is one of my better qualities.'

His low laugh held superiority as well as amusement. 'Perhaps over a lifetime I'll find out what the rest of them are. Meanwhile, I hope you can endure the five-hour flight without me to entertain you, because I have business to attend to. When I came to Sydney I hadn't planned on getting married quite so quickly. The process has taken up time that was scheduled for other matters.'

The jet had taken off while they talked. Jared unbuckled his seatbelt and lifted a briefcase on to the table in front of him.

'Is there anything I can do to help?' Laura asked.

He lifted a bundle of papers out of the case then cast her a withering look. 'I doubt you're trained for this kind of work, Laura.'

'You're making assumptions again,' she retorted. 'Besides, I'm your partner, remember?'

He laughed—without amusement—and mockingly gestured for her to join him at the table. 'By all means cast your eyes over these contracts. That's what we are committed to delivering to Singapore. And there is nothing less than an act of God that will stop me. Not even...' he looked at her with complete steadiness of purpose '...not even marriage to you.'

Laura had no intention of interfering with either his diamond or cattle business, but she was interested in finding out more about it. She ignored the bland indifference emanating from Jared and settled herself at the table. He totally ignored her presence and concentrated grimly on his paperwork.

Laura found some of the figures on the contracts absolutely staggering. No wonder Jared hadn't blinked an eyelid over offering five million dollars for her father's painting! He probably had that many cows as well as everything else! Laura did some quick mental arithmetic. The mine had to be incredibly profitable.

She tried to remember what she had read about it—established in the nineteen-seventies, it was the remnant of an extinct volcano. The carbon pushed up in its molten state had eventually crystallised into diamonds. Some were highly coloured because of the inclusion of trace elements. The same thing applied to the Argyle Diamond Mine which was also located in the Kimberley.

Laura had no idea how deep and extensive the diamond deposits were at Bendeneer. Perhaps no one knew. But Laura was sure now that it was her father who had located them. Probably in partnership with Rafe

Carellan. That was certainly indicated from what Rafe had said yesterday.

Laura started piecing together all the bits of information she had gleaned. The mine and Jared's property were both called Bendeneer. Naomi had lived on the isolated cattle station, presumably with Jared's father. Then along had come Rafe Carellan and Drew McKenzie. The open-house hospitality of the Australian outback would have been extended to them while they prospected the area. If the diamond deposits had been found on Bendeneer Downs—which seemed most probable—their discovery would have affected all of them. Perhaps it had precipitated the dreadful things that had happened.

Naomi was the centre of it all—that was obvious. One beautiful woman who craved a different sort of life, who craved company and attention, who had needs that her husband couldn't or wouldn't supply...and three men who all held out different choices for her.

Jared's father—a hard, uncompromising man—who was probably more wedded to the land than to his wife, and who wanted no other life but what he already had.

Rafe—gentle, kind, compassionate—but not in the running as far as physical attraction went.

And her own father—who had to have been someone very special for her mother to have completely lost her head over him. Had Naomi lost her head over him too? And her heart?

What build-up of pressures had led to the fight which had ended with the death of Jared's father? She didn't know, and, given the circumstances of her marriage, she could hardly ask. Yet it was obvious that Naomi and Rafe had lived haunted lives ever since. Naomi, particularly, was still traumatised by a sense of guilt. Had she played one man against the other...and lost them both in the horror of what had happened? Had she turned on Drew when she saw her husband dead... unable to bear the outcome of her own manoeuvring?

Laura dragged her mind off musing over the past. That wasn't going to help her with Jared, except in so far as it gave her an understanding of why he thought she wouldn't stick it out at Bendeneer Downs. He saw her as a beautiful woman, and clearly all his experience of beautiful women led him to believe they wanted people indulging and admiring them all the time, and they couldn't be happy outside a glittering social life. He didn't yet realise that she didn't need people around her, and superficial admiration meant less than nothing to her. But he would learn. Eventually. Time was on her side now that she was his wife. And the thought of living with Jared in a world of their own brought a sweet smile of satisfaction to her lips.

'I see our trading figures give you pleasure,' he remarked derisively.

Laura was still holding one of the larger contracts. 'How much does the mine produce, Jared?' she asked curiously, ignoring his taunt.

'About thirty million carats of diamonds a year.' The green eyes were hard as he mockingly added, 'Does that satisfy your greed?'

'Don't throw that in my face, Jared,' she shot back at him. 'You could have left those diamonds where my father found them. In the ground.'

His face tightened. 'The decision to mine them was not taken by me. I was only a boy at the time.'

'But you didn't turn your back on the mine once it was there. So why deride me for taking an interest in it now?' she argued.

'Would you have preferred to leave them in the ground, Laura?' he mocked.

'They don't matter to me, one way or the other,' she declared, staring straight back at him with steady eyes.

'But, as I am your wife, your business is my business, Jared, and I don't intend being shut out of it. No matter what nasty motive you choose to give me.'

'You expect me to believe you would have made the moves you've made if there were no diamond mine?' he demanded sceptically.

'If there were no diamond mine, would you have married me?' she retorted.

His face slowly relaxed into a sardonic smile. 'Perhaps. You are more than just a pretty face.' His eyes suddenly simmered with something more than appreciation of her ability to fight him on equal terms. 'Although I might have done other things if I hadn't seen the painting first,' he said with dry whimsy.

'Perhaps,' Laura returned just as drily, but her heart was racing with excitement. This was his first real admission that he had seen her as desirable that first night. And she wanted him to make love to her. She smiled, her eyes teasing his self-assurance. 'You might have been disappointed. You're right that I'm not just a face. But I'm not just a body either.'

'Rest assured I now have a healthy respect for the mind that drives it,' he said with heavy irony.

Her smile broadened with satisfaction. 'All I have to do now is get you interested in my personality, and we will almost have a complete person.'

She sensed his conscious retreat from her even before he spoke. 'The land will do that for me,' he said tersely. 'It brings out the best and worst in everyone.'

'And you don't think I'll pass that test?' she challenged, desperately wanting to respark his interest.

His mouth twisted. 'You heard my mother. You'll soon be bored out of your mind.'

That evidence was too hard to fight when she could offer no evidence on her own behalf. 'We'll see,' she said non-committally.

'Yes. We shall.' His eyes glittered at her with some indefinable emotion, then he bent his concentration back to his paperwork, deliberately excluding her.

The Jared Easterns of this world, Laura thought, did not give in easily. Once they made their minds up they were as immovable as rock. Or diamonds, as the case may be. But she didn't feel affronted by his dismissal. She hadn't interrupted him. It was he who had opened the conversation with her, and she had scored some points with it. Some things could not be hurried. Like respect. She was content to wait for the next opening.

Eventually Jared ordered lunch to be served and he put his work aside while they ate a lobster salad accompanied by a bottle of champagne.

'Don't you drink anything else?' Laura asked.

'You can have whatever you want,' he countered.

Laura shrugged. 'But you prefer champagne.'

'The advantage of that particular wine,' he said sardonically, 'is that the worst of it is very good, and the level of quality ascends from there to the absolutely magnificent. I always enjoy it.'

'Even at Bendeneer Downs?'

He flashed her an amused look. 'We have everything we want. It does have every comfort known to civilisation, as Rafe mentioned yesterday. What you do with it is your concern now—except for my couple of rooms which are untouchable to any female. But, if you wish, you can do over the rest of the house to your personal taste. Buy whatever you like. For your comfort. I'll be an interested spectator. To see what will make a home of it to you . . . what drives you . . . what turns you on . . .'

The amusement hardened into deep-seated cynicism as he added, 'Before the isolation drives you away. Or you become bored with the game you're playing.'

She ignored the last remark. 'How big is Bendeneer Downs?'

'It's a rough rectangle shape, about a hundred miles by a hundred and fifty. Fifteen thousand square miles in all, Laura. And you'll be sitting in the middle of it...nothing but timeless land all around you, as constant as it has been throughout the whole history of the world. And bit by bit it will start closing in on you, day after day after day...'

'It doesn't for you,' she countered.

'It's a man's country.' He lifted his glass in a mock salute to her.

'I think that what it needs...' with cool deliberation she reached across and took the glass from his hand, lifting it in a mock toast to him as she added '...is the right woman to control it.'

She heard the sibilant brush of breath between his lips as she downed the wine. There was something very dangerous indeed in his eyes when she passed the glass back to him. His hand closed around hers, imprisoning it, pressing his dominance.

'From the start, the one thing I have admired about you is your coolness——'

'Even in bed?' Laura tossed in provocatively.

His smile was positively satanic as he used his other hand to remove the glass from her fingers while still retaining his hold on her. 'I think, Laura Hammond——'

'Laura Eastern,' she corrected, barely keeping elation out of her voice. He wanted to take her. He was going to take her. He couldn't wait to take her. Which was what she had been wanting ever since he had woken her this morning.

'I think, Laura Eastern...' he said with biting precision '...that you need to be taught some respect...' He moved out from the table, pulled her up from her seat, and swept her along with him to the bedroom compartment. His eyes glittered with relish for the task he had set himself as he closed the door behind them. 'And, even if we are at thirty-five thousand feet, nothing's going to stop me,' he promised her.

Which was fine by Laura. She certainly didn't try to stop him. She wantonly encouraged him to teach her all the respect he could, but she really didn't have respect on her mind by the time they were finally sated with lovemaking. More like awe that they were so incredibly attuned to each other, and that the pleasure she had known with him last night was definitely repeatable. But she didn't tell Jared that. She didn't want to say anything that might spoil his satisfaction.

Jared didn't say anything about respect either. Eventually he pushed himself away from her, off the bed and on to his feet. He stared down at her and gave a slight shake of his head. 'I don't understand you, or what you're about, or why you're acting the way you do. I certainly don't trust you, and I never will. But I will say this for you. Tangling with you is one hell of an experience.'

The admission intensified Laura's satisfaction, but she repressed the impulse to lay her true feelings bare to possible mockery. She gave him a slow, languid smile. 'You're not too bad yourself, Jared. I've had worse.'

A sound that was very much like a growl issued from his throat and he turned aside to pick up his clothes.

Laura didn't feel like moving yet. She stretched out, enjoying the delicious sense of languor in her limbs, and savouring the smooth co-ordination of Jared's muscular body as he pulled his clothes back on. He did it with an air of dogged determination, and Laura luxuriated in the thought that he didn't want to leave her. He was forcing himself to. He paused in the doorway to look back at her, a taut, driven expression on his face, and

something in his eyes—a flicker of hungry possess-
iveness?—that made Laura's heart leap with hope.

'You have an hour before the plane lands. And I have
work to finish. Please yourself what you do,' he said
curtly, then stepped into the next compartment, pulling
the door shut behind him.

But she wouldn't let him keep putting doors between
them, Laura vowed. One by one she was going to break
them down. Even if it took the rest of her life!

CHAPTER NINE

FROM the Lear Jet, Laura's first view of the mine was disappointing. It was a tiny, lonely scar on an arid landscape, as disembodied and ugly as a crater on the moon. Yet people had fought and died because of it . . . with the passions that only a woman could stir. Somehow it couldn't excite Laura at all. If the diamonds had never been found, perhaps she would have met her father . . . known him.

'The jewel in the crown,' Jared mocked. 'I'll have someone show you the contents of the security vaults after we land.'

Laura turned her head away from the window and met the hard glitter of his green eyes with a quiet determination that she would allow nothing to shake. 'I'll wait until you want to show them to me, Jared. I'm far more interested in seeing where we live first. That's more important to me.'

His eyebrows lifted in obvious scepticism but he accepted her word without argument. 'In that case, I'll instruct the pilot to go on to the homestead airstrip.'

Laura returned her gaze to the landscape below. It reminded her of other landscapes she had seen that were starved of water: Nevada and Arizona, Zimbabwe in Africa . . .

'How many head of cattle do you run on Bendeneer Downs?' Laura asked as Jared returned to his seat.

'Depending on conditions, it varies from a hundred thousand up.'

Laura frowned. It seemed a very low figure. 'That's only about six for every square mile,' she said questioningly.

'It's a very dry country,' he drawled. 'In the drought years that's all we can feed. But the herd naturally increases in the good years. That's why we have regular musters. To brand the calves and cull out the wild bulls.' He gave her a sardonic smile. 'Not the kind of life you expected as my wife, is it?'

'What expectations I had, Jared, have been more than met,' she replied truthfully. 'Now I want more.'

His eyes narrowed. 'More of what?'

'More of you.' She gave him a wide open smile. 'Why else do you think I'm here?'

'God knows!' he muttered grimly.

His scepticism about her motives was going to be difficult to shake, but, satisfied that she had made some inroads on it, Laura once more turned her attention to the view below.

The plane was rapidly descending now and Laura's first impression of the Bendeneer Downs homestead was of a small town. Isolated it might be, but the loneliness that Jared had spoken of was definitely qualified. Obviously it comprised a community of people who would provide some company.

The size of the place made it look very prosperous. And backed by the wealth of the mine, it had to be. Everything seemed neatly organised: squares of fenced stockyards, rows of buildings with galvanised iron roofing, a great many strategically placed water-tanks, pipelines running up from a large waterhole that had been dammed from a creek, avenues of shade trees. Whatever the life was like here, she would adjust to it, Laura vowed, smiling confidently at Jared as they touched down on the airstrip.

The first people Laura saw when she and Jared stepped out of the plane were a group of boys—all Aborigines—perched on a nearby fence and waving madly at them with huge grins on their faces. Laura waved back, and in the next instant they were off the railings and scampering away, up towards the houses.

'Who are they?' she asked Jared.

'The children of our stockmen. Part of Charlie Biraban's extended family. They were here before the white man ever colonised this country. As far as I'm concerned, this is their home.' He gave Laura a hard warning look. 'This is where they stay. For life.'

'Of course,' she quickly agreed. 'That's only right.'

His eyes probed hers with sharp intensity. 'No racial prejudice?'

'Not where I come from,' she replied without the slightest hesitation. She tucked her arm around his and saw the tension ease from his face. Laura felt as though she had passed a test, even if it were a relatively minor one.

'You could try looking as if you're in love with me,' she suggested. 'It creates a good first impression.'

He gave a low laugh, and as a Jeep came screaming to a halt at the bottom of the steps he pulled her arm even more firmly around his. He even projected a lovingly indulgent manner as he introduced her to the driver.

'Laura, this is Harry Donovan, who's our full-time manager here. His wife, Gwen, manages what he doesn't.'

Harry was well into his fifties, a lean, wiry man whose weather-beaten face was creased in friendliness. His hair was iron-grey, his eyes a bright blue, and his smile beamed an unconditional welcome. Laura shook the hand that was promptly offered to her. 'I'm very pleased to meet you, Mr Donovan.'

'American?' he remarked in surprise, then in quick recovery, 'I hope you'll be happy here with us, Mrs Eastern.'

'Thank you. I'm sure I will be,' Laura said warmly, then added with a smile, 'Americans like a challenge too, you know.'

Harry Donovan gave an approving grin. 'I didn't reckon Jared would pick a non-stayer, Mrs Eastern.'

Laura's suitcase was packed in the Jeep while Harry chattered on about how delighted everyone was with the news. Apparently Jared had sent word ahead. Harry informed them that, except for those already out at the muster camps, every man, woman and child on Bendeneer Downs was up at the big house waiting to meet the woman the boss had married.

And look her over, Laura thought with a flutter of nerves. She worried briefly about her choice of clothes, then sternly reminded herself that she didn't want people responding to her clothes, but to the person she was. And everyone was ready to like her because she was Jared's wife. Nevertheless, she was very aware that this was another test she had to pass if she was to win Jared's respect.

Laura was too preoccupied with the task ahead of her to take in everything as the Jeep travelled up the road between the buildings. Stables, barns, houses all built of chamfer boards and painted a rust-red with white trim... they impressed themselves briefly on her consciousness until she caught sight of the big house. And it was certainly big!

The main body of the building had to be about a hundred and twenty feet long, and the two wings of its U-shape accounted for another sixty feet on either side. A wide veranda ran all around it, its white balustrade featuring 'Union Jack' bracing, and every veranda post carried a fancy timber moulding at the roofline. Below the veranda was a garden strip of flourishing shrubs and under the two huge pepperina trees which flanked the front steps were white wheelbarrows overflowing with a brilliant show of geraniums.

Somehow its vast sprawling design seemed to match the country on which it sat. It had a dignity, a sense of lasting timelessness about it that had an instant and deep appeal to Laura, but she had little time to contemplate it. A crowd of people were lined up on the veranda and excited greetings were called out to her and Jared as the Jeep came to a halt in front of them.

The next hour was an exhausting one for Laura. She was introduced to some fifteen families and she tried hard to remember the names and the various occupations of all the adults: mechanic, governess, book-keeper, horse-breaker, cook, and on and on...white faces and black and every shade in between, all expressing a friendly welcome. Jared, to her intense relief and pleasure, gave her every support, exhibiting the quiet pride expected of a newly-wed and doting husband. However, as soon as the courtesies were over, he stated that he and Harry had business to discuss, and he smoothly passed Laura over to the care of Gwen Donovan, Harry's wife, who was instructed to show her through the house.

Laura bit back a protest and hid her disappointment that Jared didn't see fit to show her through the house himself. Now was not the time to make a stand with so many other people around, but sooner or later she would make him recognise that this was her home as well as his, and she wasn't going to be fobbed off out of his life with such pastimes as interior decoration. She was going to be his partner in every sense there was. In the meantime, she did need to get her bearings. And make friends with Gwen Donovan, since Harry's wife undoubtedly knew all the things that Laura had to learn about.

The older woman was eager to be as accommodating as possible and Laura quickly warmed to her cheerful personality as they toured the house. Gwen was as proud of it as if it were her own. Which it was in a way. She and Harry lived in the western wing.

'How long have you been at Bendeneer Downs, Gwen?' Laura asked.

Gwen was a big-boned, solid woman who wore her age well. Her thick grey hair was pulled back into a no-nonsense bun and her strong, handsome face had the look of a person who was very comfortable with her life.

'Oh, must be over twenty years now,' she replied with a reminiscent smile. 'Our sons were only youngsters like Jared when Mr Carellan offered us the management of the place. He always used to bring Jared up from Perth for his school holidays but never stayed himself. Harry and I were born and bred in the Kimberley. We love the life here. So does Jared. But his mother...'

Gwen shook her head in a bemused fashion. 'Do you know, she's never been back...all these years. I suppose you either love it or hate it.' She frowned and darted an anxious glance at Laura. 'I guess you'll find it very different from your life in America.'

Laura laughed, more in relief than amusement. She was glad that the Donovans had not been at Bendeneer with Jared's father. They probably knew about what had happened, but Laura didn't want the past hanging over her head here. This was her and Jared's life and any intrusion of that old tragedy was no longer welcome.

'Very different,' she replied. 'But that doesn't mean I won't love it, Gwen. I love everything about this house already.'

It was not an exaggeration. The rooms were big and airy, the furniture more designed for comfort than for elegance, but very pleasing to the eye nevertheless. There were some beautiful antiques in the living-room—highly polished, solid pieces that added to the sense of permanence that seemed to characterise everything. Most of the floors were polished boards, but the various rugs that graced them were of very good quality and added a cosy charm. Laura didn't see anything she wanted to change.

The kitchen was vast and incredibly well equipped with every modern convenience. 'How does everything run?' Laura asked wonderingly. 'I mean, where does the electricity come from?'

'There are huge underground generators,' Gwen explained. 'We're luckier than most people on the land. We don't have to stint on anything here. Jared sees to that.'

Every comfort of civilisation, he had claimed, and Laura didn't find anything wanting anywhere. However, there was one over-provision that she didn't care for at all. She and Jared had separate bedrooms, linked by a common bathroom and dressing-room. When Gwen finally left her to settle in by herself, Laura did some serious rethinking about her position.

The separation of the bedrooms seemed to be symptomatic of the separation of responsibilities at Bendeneer Downs. The division of labour was very definitely drawn. The women ran the homestead community; the men worked with the cattle. Of course, one supported the other, and in the normal course of events Laura would have little quarrel with the system, but this was no normal marriage she had with Jared.

She wouldn't be able to develop the sense of working together unless she did something that would be of very real value to him. Something positive that met the challenge of the land itself. That was what he cared about. That was his pleasure. Controlling the uncontrollable,

Jared had called it. If she didn't come up with some workable plan that would really impress him, he would keep her on the periphery of his life—just a convenient woman—and she desperately wanted to be at the heart of everything. With him.

She took a shower and changed into her pink trouser-suit in deference to the fact that this would be their first dinner in their real home. Her suitcase of clothes made little impact in the cupboards in the dressing-room, and she made a mental note to ask her mother to send out the rest of her wardrobe. Then she went into Jared's bedroom to wait for him.

There would be no sense of togetherness at all if Jared insisted on keeping to separate bedrooms. That had to be settled before anything else and the time to do it was right now. It was only a few minutes before she heard him coming along the veranda, and her pulse instantly quickened. She had made a fair fist of regulating what happened between them so far and she couldn't afford to let him make all the rules at this critical point. Acting on sheer instinct, she sprawled across the bed in a pose of relaxed patience.

The moment Jared entered the room, his whole body stiffened at sight of her. 'This is my room, Laura,' he said curtly. 'You've got your own. I told you there were some things you couldn't have. This is one of them. So if you're figuring on changing anything about, forget it!'

'I was just trying out the bed to see which was more comfortable for us to sleep in,' she said reasonably. 'Or were you figuring on sleeping alone, Jared?'

His mouth twisted. 'Like you, I intend to take what I can out of this marriage. As long as it lasts. The bed you can share, whenever you like. Just don't interfere with anything else in this room. Not now. Not when I'm away. Never. Is that understood?'

'There are a couple of things you should understand, Jared,' she began purposefully.

His lips thinned. 'Don't try me too far, Laura. I've given you free rein to do what you like with the rest of the house. With the exception of my study which is also my private domain——'

'That's not what I mean,' she cut in. 'I don't intend to be here when you're away, Jared. Wherever you go, I'm going with you.'

His eyes flashed with derisive determination. 'That, my dear, is your prerogative on any trips I have to take. But you're not coming on muster with me. For one thing, I don't take any passengers in the helicopter during the round-up. It's too dangerous. I need total concentration. There's always the risk that the engine might stall on some of the close manoeuvres. And secondly, you'd only be a liability on the ground. Apart from the distraction to the men who have to keep their minds on the job, I doubt you could sit in a saddle day after day without causing everyone concern over your well-being.'

He didn't wait for any reply. He headed straight into the bathroom and shut another door between them. Laura repressed the impulse to chase after him and argue. She didn't have good enough arguments to refute what he had just said. She hadn't even known that he mustered cattle by helicopter, although she could see now how useful it would be when there was such a vast territory to cover. Perhaps she could learn to fly one. It was one item to think about.

As for the riding, Jared was right about that. Although she knew how to handle a horse and had had a fair amount of experience in the saddle...day after day was certainly out at the moment. However, by the time the next muster came around, she would be ready for that, Laura determined. And the men would know her by then, so she wouldn't be so much of a distraction.

So she had something definite to work towards, Laura reasoned, but it still wasn't enough. Probably she needed to familiarise herself with the whole picture of how the cattle station ran before she would be able to come up with any fruitful ideas.

'Regretting your decision now that you're here?'

Laura had been so deep in thought that the mocking question startled her. Jared had already washed and was emerging from the dressing-room, buttoning the cuffs of a clean shirt. His eyes were intensely watchful, waiting for any tell-tale reaction from her.

She smiled and rolled off the bed, deciding to close the physical gap between them if nothing else. 'No regrets, Jared. Just sifting through a few problems.' She walked straight up to him and began sliding her hands up his chest, her eyes teasing at the guarded reserve in his. 'I'd hate to spoil the united front we put on in front of your employees this afternoon. So tell me, Jared. What do you expect of me as your wife?'

'I have no expectations of you, Laura. Except perhaps for you to cost me as dearly as possible,' he said sardonically. His hands grasped her hips, halting any further movement towards him. 'But I will minimise that, of course, as far as it's in my power.'

'Are you frightened of me, Jared?'

Something savage flickered in his eyes. 'I've never been frightened of a woman,' he bit out scathingly. 'Certainly not.'

'Then why are you holding me away from you?'

His jaw tightened as though he was clenching his teeth. 'Don't think I can't do without you, Laura.'

'You don't have to do without me, Jared. I'm your wife,' she reminded him softly.

He gave a harsh laugh. 'Then let's see you play your loving role through dinner, my darling.'

'That's no more hardship for me than it was for you this afternoon,' she blithely declared.

She showed him so, much to the Donovans' delight. Jared had invited them to share the meal with them in the beautiful dining-room. Laura didn't have to act. It was a heady pleasure to reveal quite openly how she felt about her husband. And there were moments when she was sure that even Jared was uncertain whether she was genuine or not. He did not quibble when she suggested they retire early, and the manager and his wife were very understanding about its having been a long day. Especially since Jared had to be up before dawn the next morning.

Every step along the veranda was electric with tension, and there was no question at all about going to separate bedrooms. The door to Jared's room was the closest. Laura was swept inside with him and crushed in an embrace that throbbed with uncontrollable desire.

'Witch! Pagan!'

The words hissed from his lips as they claimed hers, but they lost any sting in the passion that surged between them. Laura didn't care what he called her as long as he no longer held back from her. But he did, for one tantalising moment when he had driven her to a quivering pinnacle of screaming need...

'Say you've never had it better! Say it!' he demanded, his voice strained in the extremity of his own need. 'Say you've never had a man like me before in your life!'

'Never...never...never...' she cried, conceding the truth without a second's thought. She was beyond thinking. She barely heard his hoarse cry of triumph as he took her to another peak of exquisite sensation, and another...

How much later it was when they lay quietly entwined, Laura didn't know. She wondered what had driven Jared to force that admission from her? Ego?

Pride? Or was it more than that? She couldn't bear to think of any other woman making him feel more than she did. Perhaps he needed to think the same of her...and if so...she wasn't just a convenience any more. She was much more special than that.

But still it was only a physical thing. She had to reach further...make Jared see she was capable of matching him in every way.

And then the idea came to her! She would have to investigate it and see if it was possible. And she needed money. Maybe a lot of money.

Memories came flooding back. One night on a veld in Zimbabwe, camping out with the group from the Peace Corps, lying in her sleeping-bag, a brilliant sky of stars, and the dark shapes that had moved past them throughout the night. The names came back to her as she remembered asking about them...Tuli, Boran, Brahman, buffalo...

Laura snuggled contentedly in Jared's arms. She didn't need to do any further investigations. She already knew enough to act. It was fear of failure when nothing was attempted that was *real* failure. If she fell on her face, so what? If it couldn't be done, so what? The attempt was everything. There were no guarantees.

To control the uncontrollable—that was what Jared was about. So, the greater the hurdle, the greater the challenge, the more she had to achieve, the more Jared should admire and respect her. That, at least, was the theory. Tomorrow, Laura determined, she would put that theory into practice.

CHAPTER TEN

A BEEPING sound impinged on Laura's sleep. A cosy warmth was withdrawn from her body and she wriggled around, trying to find it again. The noise stopped. She was still moving discontentedly when she felt bedclothes being tucked around her. It jolted her into wakefulness, just in time to see a dark silhouette moving towards the bathroom.

'Jared!'

'Go back to sleep, Laura.'

'Is it time for you to leave?'

'Yes. If you didn't want to be disturbed, you should have gone to your own room.'

'I don't recall you suggesting that last night.'

'No. But since you have such a strong mind of your own I didn't think I needed to,' he retorted sardonically.

'I wanted to be woken up. I want you to organise something for me before you leave,' she said quickly.

'Tell me when I'm dressing. I'll consider it then,' he said autocratically.

She hitched herself up on the pillows, switched on the bedside lamp, and wondered how best to word her request while she waited until he had finished in the bathroom. Straight to the point, she decided. It didn't matter how she put it, he would think the worst of her anyhow. Until she proved he was wrong.

He came out of the dressing-room, already dressed in shirt and jeans, but he carried socks and boots. Laura hoped he would sit on the bed to put them on, but he dropped into a chair on the other side of the room, keeping a very emphatic distance between them.

'What is it you want?' he asked curtly.

'I want my own private bank account with a hundred thousand dollars in it,' she stated unequivocally.

He flashed her an acid look. 'So now it starts. I'm only surprised you're asking for so little.'

'You could be right. Stupid to be niggardly. Make it half a million dollars, Jared.' Laura was sure she wouldn't need that much, but he deserved some pain for thinking bad thoughts about her.

'Half a million should cover quite a bit of interior decoration,' he said sarcastically. 'What do you intend? Covering the walls in gold?'

'Actually I was thinking of something exterior rather than interior. And another thing. I want to learn how to fly a helicopter.'

He looked up sharply from pulling on a boot. 'Why?'

'Why not? You can fly one. I want to too. Maybe you know someone who could teach me.'

He finished pulling on the boot and started on the second one. 'I'll teach you myself when I have the time,' he said gruffly.

Laura felt a thrill of triumph that he was actually offering to spend time with her. She was making real progress now! 'That would be marvellous, Jared. Thank you,' she said warmly.

He shot her a wary look as he stood up. 'Is that all, Laura?'

'You will fix up about the money? I do want to get started on my project straight away.'

'What project?' he asked suspiciously.

'Nothing for you to worry about. I promise I won't spoil anything. And I'd like it to be a surprise,' she said, smiling brightly at him.

He drew in a deep breath. 'Whatever makes you happy,' he said with an ironic twist. 'Just make sure it doesn't make me unhappy. I'll speak to Harry. He'll get it arranged first thing today.' The last words were tossed at her as he headed for the doors which led on to the veranda.

'Jared!'

'What now?' he snapped at her.

Laura flung off the bedclothes and ran to him, throwing her arms around his neck before he could make any move to stop her. 'You're not going without kissing me goodbye, are you, Jared?'

'Laura! For God's sake! This is no time for playing games!' There was a ragged edge to his vehemence, and his hands were curving around her soft, warm nakedness as she hung on and insinuated her body even more intimately against his.

'One kiss won't hurt you, Jared,' she pleaded, thrusting her fingers persuasively through his thick tan-gold hair. 'And I was a very good wife last night, wasn't I?'

His chest heaved and his mouth crashed down on hers in angry compliance. But the kiss didn't stay angry. Like the way he moved his hands over her, it was hungrily possessive, and when he finally wrenched his head up, a raging conflict glittered in his eyes.

'I've got to go. And I'm going,' he enunciated with biting determination. He thrust her away from him and held her at arm's length. 'Goodbye... my wife! I'll see you in a week's time. If you're still here.'

He banged the door shut after him. His footsteps fairly thundered along the veranda, almost as if the hounds of hell were snapping at his heels. Laura grinned to herself and leapt back into Jared's bed, snuggling under the bedclothes in sensuous delight. He was her man all right. And she would soon convince him that she was his woman.

Already he wanted her to stay with him. Or at least still be here for him when he came back. He wouldn't have offered to teach her to fly a helicopter otherwise. And he hadn't really blinked about the money. Whatever makes you happy—those were his exact words. She simply had to teach him that what would make her happiest was sharing everything with him.

She drifted back to sleep and didn't wake again until almost eight o'clock, by which time Jared was long gone on his mustering. Nevertheless, not even his absence could dim her excitement as she got herself ready to face her first morning at Bendeneer Downs. Life was suddenly full of beautiful possibilities.

It was hot already, but not the humid heat of Port Douglas where her father had lived out his years. It was dry outback heat that was actually far more bearable than the coastal tropics. Laura dressed in shorts and a loose shirt. She strapped sturdy Roman sandals to otherwise bare feet, swept her hair up in a pony-tail, and almost danced out on to the veranda.

The delicious smell of freshly baked bread wafted in the air. The shouts of children mingled with the barks of dogs. Laura didn't feel the least bit isolated. Bendeneer Downs was like a small kingdom, and Jared's people were her people. No way would she be lonely or bored here!

She found Gwen Donovan in the kitchen with the two Aboriginal girls who helped in the house—Susie and Sally. Laura insisted on having her breakfast at the kitchen table so she could chat to them all, but the girls were full of shy giggles so it was Gwen who answered her questions.

'I thought you must be baking bread,' Laura remarked questioningly, looking around at the ovens although there was no smell of it in the kitchen.

'Down in the bake-house,' Gwen explained. 'I'll show you after you've eaten. If you like.'

'Yes, please. I'm looking forward to seeing everything,' Laura said eagerly.

Gwen laughed. 'And everyone's looking forward to strutting their stuff in front of you, Laura. They'll probably talk your ears off.'

Susie served her a dish of fresh fruit: melons and papaw and banana all neatly diced. 'Do we fly these in?' she asked.

'Good lord, no!' Gwen exclaimed with another laugh. 'We're fairly self-sufficient here. Grow all our own fresh fruit and vegetables. The soil is very good. It's the lack of water that's the problem. But Jared has that solved around the homestead. Would you like some eggs to follow the fruit? We keep poultry too.'

She went on to tell Laura about the meat-house and the store where all dried and tinned foods were kept, as well as a stock of clothes and other maintenance necessities. A bell started ringing loud and clear and Gwen immediately answered Laura's unspoken question.

'The school bell. It's nine o'clock.'

'How many children do we have of school age?'

'Fourteen this year. In five different grades. So Jill—our governess—really has to juggle them around for the School of the Air sessions.'

'What's School of the Air?'

'Lessons by radio. They're beamed out by teachers at Derby. That's the closest town on the west coast.'

Laura shook her head in amazement. She had heard of the Flying Doctor service, but School of The Air was completely new to her. She was intrigued to see how it worked.

'It only goes up to the sixth grade,' Gwen explained. 'After that the children have to go to boarding school to further their education. Some of them won't leave home, and Jared doesn't force them to. But he arranges for them to be taught practical skills here on the station. Susie's brother, Bill, is a marvellous mechanic. He can fix anything.'

'Sally's got her eye on Bill,' Susie declared, and both girls burst into another fit of giggles.

Gwen sent them off to clean rooms while she took Laura on a grand tour of the places she had spoken about.

Bread was baked every second day. The store was open every morning for anyone who needed anything. The radio lessons were very personal, each child speaking to the teacher in turn. The meat-house looked as if it could feed the whole community for weeks.

Laura reacquainted herself with most of the people she had met yesterday and thoroughly enjoyed herself with everyone. Their last stop was at the stables where she arranged with Tim, the head stable-boy, to have a very tame horse ready for her to ride later in the afternoon.

They returned to the big house for lunch, and Laura took the opportunity to ask Harry if she might have a private chat with him in Jared's study. Harry didn't go on muster any more. He had a back problem that was aggravated by riding long hours, so he contented himself with doing all the organising and handling the business end of fulfilling contracts.

Jared's study was a very masculine room: a massive oak desk, dark brown leather armchairs, an olive-green rug on the floor. Against one wall was a large showcase of trophies, and above it hung an impressive number of blue ribbons from cattle shows. Wall-to-wall book-shelves held rows of magazines and books, and there were several businesslike filing cabinets under the window behind the desk.

'I called the accountant at the mine, Laura,' Harry informed her as soon as they were settled. 'He'll have that money available for your use before today's over.'

'Thank you, Harry. I shouldn't need anywhere near that much...'

'But Jared wouldn't want you to be wanting,' he finished with a grin. 'Now what else can I do for you? You have a special project in mind, Jared said.'

The slight embarrassment about the money faded as she realised how easy Jared had made it for her to enlist Harry's help. 'Yes, I have,' she leapt in eagerly. 'Something I want to try. An experiment that might work out well here. And if we don't try, we'll never know, will we? Do the names Tuli and Boran mean anything to you, Harry?'

He shook his head. 'Can't say they do.'

Laura plunged on, fired by the hope that her plan could be a success. 'They're breeds of cattle in Africa. Something like Brahman, only even more resistant to heat and disease. Anyhow, I know they breed them in Zimbabwe because I've seen them there. And the thing about them is, they can survive longer in drought conditions than any other breed because they've got well-developed sweat glands. They're more fitted to this country than English herds. I think we'll get increased reproduction and growth rates from them. And what I want to do is import a bull and a small herd of cattle. We can fence off a part of Bendeneer Downs where they can graze without mixing with the herd here, and see how they make out.'

Harry looked dumbfounded. He slowly shook his head as if needing to clear cobwebs out of his brain. 'I thought...' He paused, made a helpless little gesture with his hands, then gave her a lop-sided smile. 'Looks to me like Jared's got himself one hell of a wife. Does he know about this?'

Laura decided that discretion was definitely the better part of valour at this point. 'Jared said I could go ahead and do anything that makes me happy. He gave me a free hand. And this is what I want to do, Harry.'

He chuckled, his blue eyes crinkling with amused delight. 'Don't get me wrong, Laura. I'm with you all the way. There's just not too many women—or men, for that matter—who'd come up with an idea like this. New...radical...innovative...and it sure sounds good to me. Well worth a try. Even if it doesn't work.'

'Thank you, Harry.' Laura breathed a deep sigh of satisfaction. 'And for the moment, let's keep it completely to ourselves. I don't even know if it's possible to do it. I need your advice on what channels I have to go through. Government boards or special departments?'

'I'll get straight on to it. One thing's certain. Whatever you bring over will have to be quarantined. It's not going to be quick, Laura. You'll have to be patient.'

'Then you'll make enquiries for me? Get the ball rolling?'

'Right away,' he promised. 'I'll certainly have some workable information by tonight.'

'You're a marvel, Harry!' Laura exclaimed with very sincere fervour.

He laughed outright. 'I reckon you're the marvel around here, Laura. Now I know how Jared got poleaxed. All these years women didn't seem to mean anything to him. But you...' Again he shook his head. 'Well, good luck to you, my dear! And good luck to him. Glad to see it.'

Laura wished it was as easy to convince Jared of that as it was Harry, but she was well pleased with the success of the initiative she had taken. Harry was now her firm ally, and together they would get the project active as soon as possible. Hopefully, before Jared got back from his muster. She wanted something definite in hand to show him she would be a true partner to him.

Luck was certainly on her side. Harry informed her that night that the CSIRO department was actually running an experimental operation on the Cocos Islands, importing frozen embryos of the breeds she had named from Zimbabwe and impregnating Friesian cows from Australia with them. Graziers from Queensland were supporting the experiment. She might be able to buy out a share . . . for the right price. Otherwise she would have to put in her order and wait another eighteen months.

'We've got half a million dollars, Harry. Let's buy whatever we can with that,' Laura instructed without a moment's hesitation.

The days that followed were packed with activity for Laura. Most mornings she spent with Harry, pressing for a resolution about the cattle she wanted. A deal was finally made. Forty cows and two bulls would be air-freighted from the Cocos Islands to Bendeneer Downs within the month. While all this was being negotiated, Laura learnt a great deal about the running of the station under Harry's and Gwen's coaching. Then every afternoon she spent more and more time in the saddle.

The horse that Tim had chosen for her was a very biddable mare called Dimity, and Laura enjoyed riding her. The head stable-hand, cautious of the boss's wife's safety, always insisted that someone ride along with her, so Laura made the acquaintance of the Aboriginal boys who had waved to her from the fence that first afternoon.

She particularly liked two of them, Boodie and Johnno, who regaled her with tales of their prowess at fending for themselves on the land. They both boasted they could survive anything, anywhere, any time, and they were going to be the best stockmen ever on Bendeneer Downs. Laura was inclined to believe them.

One thing was certain—they could handle horses as though they were born on them.

The wedding photographs arrived on her fifth day at Bendeneer Downs. Jared hadn't bothered about choosing from negatives. Two large prints of every shot taken were in the packet, and they were all surprisingly good. Laura studied each one of them, and almost convinced herself that Jared *was* in love with her. But photographs could lie, and she was all too well aware of Jared's deep reservations where she was concerned.

Nevertheless, she had no doubts about sending a complete set to her mother to use or show as she wished. She wrote a long letter to accompany them, wanting her mother to understand the life she had chosen with Jared, but having little hope that she would. It was far too removed from Boston. Yet Laura yearned to recapture the brief wave of empathy they had shared on her wedding-day. She wanted to reach out to her mother again. She wished she could have reached out to her father...

The thought reminded her of the other photographs she had left in the lid-pocket of her suitcase...the ones she had taken of her father's painting. That scene had to be somewhere on Bendeneer Downs. When she went out riding that afternoon she described it to Boodie and Johnno and asked if they knew of a place like that.

'Plenty places like that, Miss Laura. You want us to show you one?' Boodie crowed in his cocksure knowledge of all the land hereabouts.

'Yes, I would,' Laura said eagerly.

'Long way to ride,' Johnno objected, very conscious of his responsibility to look after the boss's wife.

'We can point it out. Miss Laura can see,' Boodie argued. 'Then we bring her home.'

The matter was settled on this agreeable note, and it was only a little over an hour later that she saw it—the straw-pale plain dotted with baobab trees, and, towering behind it, the great range of sandstone mountains. It gave her an odd feeling to know that her father had been here before her. That this was what had lived in his memory all those lonely years. She immediately decided that tomorrow she would ride all the way and camp overnight so she could watch the sunset that he had painted. It was probably as close as she could ever get to the father she had never known.

Johnno insisted that they head back to the homestead, and, with her decision made, Laura didn't argue. It was fortunate that they did turn back then because they were still a fair ride away when they saw the helicopter coming in. Laura immediately urged her mare into a gallop. Why Jared was home two days early, she didn't know or care. She simply didn't want to miss any time with him. She raced straight up to the big house, and handed her horse over to the boys to return to the stables.

Her heart was galloping as she dashed along the veranda to Harry's office, expecting Jared to be there, talking about the muster. But only Harry and the bookkeeper were in the room.

'Jared?' she asked breathlessly.

'Gone to clean up for you,' Harry said with a wide grin.

'Did you tell him about the shipment of cattle, Harry?'

'No. I reckoned that was your news, Laura.'

'Right!'

She gave him a grateful grin then shot away to the kitchen. She wasn't too sure that Jared was actually cleaning up *for her*, but she could use the extra time to her advantage. Luckily Gwen and the two girls were in the kitchen preparing vegetables for dinner.

'Have we got any Beluga caviare, Gwen?'

'Always some in stock,' came the prompt reply.

'Then let's get it out. And a bottle of the best champagne. Do you know why Jared's home early, Gwen?'

'Maybe he just couldn't stay away from caviare and champagne,' came the arch reply, which broke the girls into hysterical giggles. 'Susie, you cut up the onion,' Gwen ordered through her own laughter. 'Sally, there are boiled eggs in the fridge. Get moving! You know what accompaniments Jared likes to have with his caviare.'

Ten minutes later Laura bore a loaded tray to Jared's room. The thought that he might have come home because he couldn't stay away from her put an extra lilt in Laura's step. But she didn't really believe it. Most probably he had run out of fuel for the helicopter...or something. Nevertheless, she was going to make the most of the occasion.

She couldn't hear water running in the bathroom so she checked to see if he was already dressing. The connecting door to her room was wide open. And Jared was standing at her writing-desk, studying one of the wedding photographs.

'They're very good, don't you think?' she said brightly.

He swung around, and for a moment there was a sharp question in his eyes, as if he had seen something in the photograph that made him wonder about her. Then his gaze dropped to the tray she was still carrying and his mouth twitched in sardonic amusement.

'Am I being welcomed home, or should I be on my guard? A Greek bearing gifts spells extreme danger.'

He wore a short black towelling bath-robe which left a deep V of his chest and his long powerful legs bare. Freshly showered and shaved, he literally exuded masculine virility, and Laura's breath was caught somewhere at the back of her throat. She fiercely wished that she had had time to clean herself up after her long, dusty ride. She was not used to worrying about her attractiveness. Hadn't even stopped to think about her appearance. And it was too late to correct the matter now. Jared was waiting for an answer. She had to get her mind back on the challenging track that made their relationship tenable. With a supreme effort she got her brain and lungs working again.

'You like facing danger, Jared, so whichever way you want to look at it this is a welcome home,' she declared.

He gave his low laugh, which made him even more compellingly attractive. 'So the charade goes on, does it?'

'I thought you photographed very well.' Laura carried the tray over to the desk, put it down, and picked up the shot he had been studying. 'My mother will certainly think you're very much in love with me.'

'I was thinking the same thing of you.' His hands slid around her waist and pulled her back against him. 'But we both know better, don't we?' he murmured into her ear, moving his lips over it with teasing sensuality.

A delicious tingle of excitement spread through Laura. Perhaps Jared really had come home because he wanted to be with her. Eager to see some need for her in his eyes, she tried to turn around, but he tightened one arm around her waist, pinning her against him.

'Stay right where you are, my little witch-wife. This time I'm running the show,' he said, and it was the need for some dominance over her that gravelled through his voice.

But as his free hand roved up over her breasts to the top button of her shirt, she felt the stirrings of his desire that no words in the world could hide or diminish, and she knew there was no dominance. Nor did she feel diminished in any way at her body's response to the exquisite caressing of her bared flesh. It was no suffering to her to be held and touched with such erotic finesse.

She did not fight the waves of pleasure that rippled through her in increasing strength, melting her bones so that it was only his support that kept her standing. It was Jared who could no longer bear not to take what she could give him. With a guttural cry he swung her around and crushed her heated flesh to his, arching back at the sheer impact of the long-deferred intimacy.

Laura didn't remember afterwards how they got to the bed. She recalled only that first sweet thrust of him inside her and the incredible storm of sensation that followed, holding him tightly when he finally collapsed on top of her, and kissing him over and over in an ecstasy of feeling that had nothing to do with power games and never would.

And when eventually he spoke, Jared made no mention of having run any show. Nor did he talk about charades. He said, with a very dry intonation, 'I think that champagne should be properly chilled by now.'

'Yes,' she agreed huskily. 'I'm not much good at opening bottles, Jared.'

He gave that low laugh that seemed to hit the pit of her stomach, then slowly untangled his limbs from hers. Laura rolled on to her back and watched him with immense pleasure as he dispensed with the cork and filled two glasses. He brought the whole tray over to the bedside table. Laura hitched herself up on the pillows as he held out one of the glasses to her.

'So...have you managed to get through the half million yet?' he asked mockingly.

'Not quite,' Laura answered, and sipped her champagne with every appearance of blithe unconcern. 'But I do have to discuss fencing with you,' she added on a more purposeful note.

'Fencing,' he repeated sardonically, and proceeded to spread a crouton with caviare. He passed it to her then made a more elaborate operation of mixing everything on to another one for his personal taste. 'What do you want to fence?' he asked before biting into it.

'Enough land to carry fifty cattle.'

The green eyes sliced to her in sharp disbelief. 'Any particular fifty cattle?' he drawled.

'Oh, yes! Very particular! They cost me a lot of money,' she said. And at the arrogantly mocking raising of his eyebrows she proceeded to tell him precisely what cattle and why she had bought them and what she intended to do with them.

The disbelief and mockery were very quickly neutralised. Calculations and speculation grew in their place, and when Laura had finished informing him of the length and breadth of her venture into cattle-breeding Jared stared at her for a long time before speaking.

'You . . . are one hell of a competitor, Laura. You're going to take me on all the way, aren't you?' His mouth twisted in dry irony. 'Though I grant you I like this investment better than gold wallpaper.'

'The name is Laura Eastern, Jared. And I'm taking this land on. Just like you. Not against you. As far as I'm concerned, your business is my business. And if there's any way of making our business better, I'm willing to try it. Do you have any argument with that?'

It was a very deliberate challenge, and on it hung the future of their relationship. If he refused to accept her interest, there could only be the most bitter conflict ahead. For what seemed an eternity the green eyes searched hers with fierce intensity.

'This is a long-term project you've embarked on, Laura,' he stated without any inflexion at all.

'I'm aware of that, Jared. I aim to see it through. But obviously I need your co-operation,' she said just as flatly.

He nodded slowly, as if feeling his way with great care. 'I would prefer, in future, that you don't make any more decisions relating to *our* business without my knowledge.'

'I would prefer, in future, to be accorded the same respect, Jared.'

His mouth twitched in dry appreciation and Laura knew she had the battle won even before he said, 'Are we now looking towards a long future, Mrs Eastern?'

Her lips curved in quiet triumph. 'I believe we are, Mr Eastern.'

He refilled her glass then tapped it with his own. 'Tangling with you grows ever more stimulating, but don't let it go to your head, Laura. Because I'll keep my head, no matter what you come up with,' he warned her mockingly, then quaffed the contents of his glass without a breath taken.

'I'd hate you to lose your head, Jared,' Laura retorted when his eyes flicked back to hers. 'It's one of the best parts of you.'

For the very first time he gave a full-throated laugh. His eyes danced at her in pure unholy joy as he took her glass from her hand and replaced it on the tray. He lifted her arms above her head and moved his body over hers with slow, sensual deliberation.

'Tell me another, you savage little pagan,' he breathed against her lips.

'Only if you let go of my arms,' she teased.

He released them, but Laura didn't tell him that what she wanted most was for him to lose his heart to her. Maybe he would always guard that too closely. But at least she was no longer a wife in status only. He had accepted her as his partner. And equal in spirit. That was more than enough to forge a solid and lasting future.

She could even start thinking of having a child...a family. After all, what was a kingdom without heirs?

Laura was sure that Jared would heartily approve of that development. He might never allow himself to love her, but Laura had no doubt at all that he would love their children.

CHAPTER ELEVEN

IT WAS the beeping horn of the Jeep that woke Laura the next morning. She and Jared had slept in her room, far too preoccupied with each other to think of setting an alarm. She heard Jared mutter something under his breath, then an arm came around her waist and scooped her back against him. Deliciously sensual kisses trailed down her shoulder as his hand glided up to her breasts, and it was more than an hour later that Laura remembered the beeping horn. The tempestuous blazing intensity of their lovemaking had blotted it completely from her mind.

Jared lay half sprawled across her naked body in a relaxed abandonment of any cares whatsoever. She tried to remonstrate with him as her fingers teased across his chest and stole slowly down his stomach. 'Your driver has been waiting a long time, Jared.'

'Mmm...' His stomach contracted under her feathering touch. 'This morning I'm sleeping in. I guess I must have been very tired.'

'Don't you feel guilty?'

'Sometimes it's worthwhile being the boss.'

'Everyone on the station will know what you've been up to.'

'Yes.'

He showed no remorse at all, and Laura couldn't help a little gurgle of laughter. Which Jared apparently found provocative, because he suddenly found the energy to silence it. Very effectively. And the driver of the Jeep had to wait a good while longer.

141

Only after he left did Laura finally stir herself to rise. Since there were another two days' work in the muster, and it was most unlikely that Jared would break his work schedule again, she was free to go ahead with her plan to return to the place her father had painted and stay overnight there. There was nothing she wanted to do more.

However, Harry and Gwen weren't too keen on her camping out overnight. 'I'm taking Boodie and Johnno with me. They'll look after me,' Laura insisted. Then to set their minds at rest she added, 'I have trekked through most of Africa, and seen quite a bit of the rest of the world—including the Kimberley. I'm experienced at looking after myself. There won't be any trouble, so you're not to worry about me,' she commanded with a confident smile.

Any objections were promptly dropped, but Harry took the precaution of getting Boodie to describe exactly where they were going.

Laura and the boys set off on their horses after lunch, giving themselves plenty of time to reach their destination before sunset. Quite an unnecessary amount of camping gear was loaded on a pack-horse which accompanied them. Apparently the boss's wife was not expected to 'rough it' on a meagre bed-roll under the stars. Rather than order that the extra comforts be unloaded, Laura silently contented herself with the thought that Johnno and Boodie would report back to everyone that Miss Laura could 'rough it' as well as anybody.

The boys were in high spirits. As they rode along they entertained Laura by identifying all the plants and wildlife they saw and telling stories about them. There was one underlying theme in everything they said: survival in a hard country. The strong lived, the weak died. There was nothing in between. Jared had told her last night how they had had to shoot a number of calves which had been found suffering from tick-poisoning. It was an act of mercy. There were no vets, no vaccines within a thousand miles. Better a quick death than a gradual deterioration which left them prey to other painful horrors.

However, as they rode further and further into the straw-pale plain her father had painted, Laura was too overwhelmed by sadness to be a good listener. The boys quickly sensed her change of mood and chatted quietly between themselves until they reached a water-hole where they advised Laura that this was the best place to camp. They dismounted, and Laura handed the reins of her horse to Johnno.

'I want to go for a walk by myself,' she said decisively. 'Will you two stay here and set up camp?'

'Sure thing, Miss Laura. We'll look after everything,' Johnno replied cheerfully.

She left them to it and walked slowly towards the giant baobab tree that had been depicted so hauntingly in the foreground of her father's painting. The weird bottle-shaped trunk, with the incredibly twisted limbs sprouting from its apex, seemed to claw at the sky in tortured longing. Had it been to her father a visual expression of his own innermost feelings—the love for another man's wife that was tearing at his soul? Had he felt a deep empathy with this land?

Tell me about him, she cried silently to the rugged sandstone range that jagged across the skyline in the distance. She trailed her hand around the trunk of the baobab tree, pressed her back against it, and stared up at the ancient mountains that had stood sentinels to untold lifetimes. She had no trouble identifying the craggy outcrop which had merged into Naomi's face. It had probably been there for centuries and would stay the same through centuries to come...indestructible...timeless. As her father's love for Naomi had been.

But he had remembered his daughter. He had talked about her to Naomi. And he had left her this...a legacy of love and pain. Tears pricked her eyes and she slid down the tree-trunk to sit at its base, suddenly tired and sick at heart. All those lonely, needing years...they might have been so close if they had known each other.

Tears gathered in force and spilled down her cheeks. Laura didn't even try to stop them. For so long she had fought her own battles, made herself self-sufficient, but there was still a child inside her that cried out to be wanted and loved, no matter what she looked like or what she was. To simply belong to someone without question or reservation. Why did her father have to die before she even heard of his existence? Couldn't he have written to her before that? Couldn't he...?

The beating sound of an approaching helicopter thumped into her overloaded heart. Her mind screamed a protest against what it meant and sought frantically to explain it away. The mustering was being done a long way from here, but Jared could be just passing over. Surely he wouldn't be coming for her. Not a second time. He didn't need her that much, and even his sexual passion must now surely be appeased.

Tension played havoc with her overstressed nerves as the noise came closer and closer. The sound built up to a crescendo, then cut out altogether. He had landed. Probably near the water-hole where the boys were setting up camp. And he would come looking for her if she didn't go to meet him. He must have already been to the homestead to have learnt where she was, and as soon as he had been told...only God knew what significance he would put on her coming here to the scene of the painting!

And Laura simply wasn't fighting fit at the moment. She was a mess; her face streaked with tears, her emotions in tatters. How was she going to cope with Jared when she wasn't even in control of herself? Any other time and place she would have welcomed Jared's company, but not here. Not now. This was an intensely private matter to her and he wouldn't under-stand...wouldn't be sympathetic...couldn't be sym-pathetic. Her father had killed his father. She had to remember that.

Even trying to explain anything seemed hopeless, but she had to cope somehow. Jared left her no other choice. Laura pushed herself to her feet and leaned against the tree-trunk as she rubbed over her face with the sleeve of her shirt. She took several deep breaths in a desperate attempt to compose herself, then took the couple of steps around the trunk that would give her a view of what was happening at the campsite.

Jared was covering the ground towards her in long, lithe strides. The lowering sun glinted on his hair, making it look golden. The workmanlike jeans and shirt did nothing to diminish his strong aura of sexuality. He came to a halt a few paces short of her, his hard warrior-face looking as if it were carved from granite, the green eyes searing hers with bitter questions, and tension ema-nating from him in a swirl that almost choked her.

'What are you doing here, Laura?' he demanded curtly. 'I thought we agreed to let the past go.'

'I'm not bringing it up, Jared,' she said in an attempt to appease the bitter accusation in the green eyes. An ungovernable wave of sadness brought another welling of tears and she half turned away as she fought for composure.

'Laura?' He sounded incredulous. A hand grasped her arm and turned her around to face him again.

'I can't help having feelings about it!' she cried in protest, unable to stop the tears from trickling down her cheeks. 'And I'm not harming anyone or anything! I know you don't have any reason to care about him,' she blurted out. 'But he was my father. And this...this is all I have of him.'

She bit her lips and shook her head, but it was as if all the bottled-up feelings of her childhood were clamouring for an outlet and the tears just kept on rolling.

'Laura...'

Her blurred vision didn't allow her to see the expression on his face, but the note of concern in his voice was her total undoing.

'Please...' she sobbed. 'Just...just let me...'

Arms encircled her. Whether they were friendly or not she didn't know or care. She was swiftly drawn into a warm haven of strength and rocklike support, caressed with a soothing tenderness, held secure while the storm within her ran its turbulent course and faded into limp exhaustion. Somehow she couldn't bring herself to be concerned about the debilitating emotion that left her dependent on Jared's compassion. It felt so good just to rest her head on his broad shoulder, to feel his cheek rubbing softly over her hair, to be wrapped in his arms, to sag against him and know he wouldn't discard her or let her fall.

The game she had played, the deception that had rolled on and on gathering a mad life of its own, the fight to survive, to keep on top, in control—somehow it had all collapsed on her...become meaningless. She wanted the truth—craved for it—whatever price had to be paid for it.

'Jared...' She didn't lift her head. Didn't want to see if she was breaking into forbidden ground. He either answered her or not. And if not...there was nothing anyway. 'Was my father...was he to blame for what happened? You said... you implied... do you truly believe that...?'

'No!' It sounded like an explosion of feeling that he had kept deeply suppressed, that hurt him to admit, yet which demanded admission. She felt his chest expand as he dragged in a deep breath and there was a note of pained searching for truth in his voice when he slowly added, 'How does one apportion blame? Who can unweave all the threads that lead to tragedy? A meshed web of circumstances. Passions driven to breaking-point...'

He sighed and his breath wavered through her hair like the soft stirring of a wind of change. The words that followed were slow and measured, weighed in the balance of what was known and unknown.

'Your father was probably no more to blame than was mine. There are some women with the power to twist men's souls. My mother is one of them. Even Rafe... poor, damned Rafe hungering for the crumbs she gave him... does give him... and I hate seeing it. I hated it then... what I felt was happening all around me... but I was only a boy, Laura. There was nothing I could do to stop it. Nothing anyone could do...'

Only a boy... caught in the middle of something he didn't understand... and his father ending up dead. A wave of sympathy for his lonely fears and the terrible loss he had suffered stirred Laura from her own anguish of soul. She lifted her head, bleak grey eyes meeting and understanding the pain in his.

'I'm truly sorry about your father, Jared,' she said softly. 'You must have been very close to him.'

The slight twist of his mouth mocked himself, not her. 'How close does anyone get to another human being? Yet, he was... everything I wanted to be. But that was a boy's point of view. A son's blind love for his father. Obviously he was not everything my mother wanted.'

'Jared...' She hesitated, aware that she was scraping over old wounds, yet her need to know pushed the plea from her lips. 'How did he die? What happened? You intimated that it wasn't an accident. That my father——'

'Laura, I don't truly know,' he confessed gently. 'A violent fight broke out between them. My mother was screaming. She ran and got a rifle. I think...to stop them. She yelled at me to fetch Rafe, who had walked away when the quarrelling started. We heard the shot. By the time we'd run inside, my father was dead, my mother was sobbing hysterically over his body, and Drew was standing there, staring down at them, the rifle in his hands. Rafe asked him what happened. He didn't answer. He just handed the rifle to Rafe and walked away. He never said a word. No explanation. He packed up and left within the hour and we never saw him again. My mother kept crying that it was an accident. She said there had been a struggle for the gun and it had gone off.'

He gave an apologetic grimace. 'The fact that Drew went away, turning his back on everything... I guess I always interpreted it as guilt. But it might have been shock, Laura.'

The kind, conciliatory tone of Jared's last suggestion floated over Laura's head. She was thinking along another line altogether. What if it had been Naomi's finger on the trigger? Drew McKenzie might well have left in order to protect the woman he had loved, taking the guilt upon himself. And Naomi might well have let him, only to be haunted by the thought of his sacrifice for her ever since.

However, there was nothing to be gained by suggesting that idea to Jared. Whatever his mother's sins, she had certainly suffered for them. Andrew McKenzie had taken his secrets to the grave and it was better all around if they remained there now. Nevertheless, Laura couldn't quite repress her unsatisfied curiosity about her father. Again her eyes lifted to Jared's in searching appeal.

'Could you tell me what my father was like? From a boy's point of view? From any point of view.'

He frowned. 'You would know better than I what he was like, Laura.'

She heaved a deep, shuddering sigh and pulled out of his embrace, feeling too uncomfortable to stay in the comfort of his arms. The wounds to both of them went too deep. Her legs felt weak and shaky so she backed up against the baobab tree and leaned against it. If there was a time when truth had to be spoken, it was now, whatever the consequences.

'I didn't know him, Jared,' she confessed. 'I never knew him. I didn't even know of him... until he was dead. Only then did I receive word of him and what he had left me.' The memory of how cheated and robbed she had felt shadowed her eyes. 'It was as if...something I had always yearned for...had been there all the time...only I wasn't told it was within reach...until it was gone.'

She swallowed down the lump of emotion that had risen in her throat. Jared was staring at her as if he had never seen her before and she desperately wanted him to understand.

'You see... I never fitted in with the life my family led in Boston. I wasn't the kind of child my mother wanted. The man I thought was my father didn't have much time for children, and I... I didn't have the assets he might have valued in a daughter. So when I found out that for all those years there had been someone who might have loved me, whom I could have belonged to, and I might have been with him if only he'd got in touch, or come to see me...'

'Laura, Drew couldn't come to you. He was a wanted man. After my father died, he never surrendered himself to the law. He simply disappeared. If he'd tried to leave Australia, chances were he would have been picked up on the manslaughter charge. Perhaps even murder,' Jared explained quietly. 'And that would have dragged my mother and the whole messy tragedy into the public eye. I don't think he could have borne to see her again. To go through it all. And he would have thought...I'm sure he did think...you were better off without him. He certainly gave up everything else.'

'I know that now,' Laura said painfully. 'I guess I knew it when I went in search of him and the life he led. The way he lived at Port Douglas was so...so bereft of any real human contact. He kept to himself. Wouldn't associate with any woman. And that painting. I knew something dreadful had happened to him...' her eyes begged his belief as she added '...but I didn't know how bad it was on your side, Jared. I truly didn't. I'm sorry. I just wanted...'

'To take from us what we had taken from you and your father,' he said as Laura floundered for words.

'No!' She shook her head, helpless to explain exactly what she had felt. 'You can't get...what's forever gone. I thought if I came here...' She looked up at the mountains. 'If I watched the sunset...'

Jared stepped forward and turned her face back to his. The green eyes questioned without any of the cynicism Laura was accustomed to seeing in them. 'You really don't care about money...or diamonds. That's not why you married me, is it?'

'No. It's not. I wanted other things, Jared. Things that I've been looking for.' Her mouth curved into a dry half-smile. 'I guess...somewhere...a place for me. And to be wanted. The driving need to be wanted...and to belong...somewhere.'

'And is this the place you want, Laura?' he asked, quietly and seriously.

'I think . . . as close as I'll ever get to it,' she answered truthfully. She couldn't make Jared love her, but he was her husband. And she was falling desperately in love with him. Certainly she didn't want to live without him.

He gently stroked the disarrayed strands of hair back from her face. He had a strange, almost whimsical look in his eyes. 'Perhaps Rafe was right,' he mused. 'And this is the resolution.'

He gave a little shake of his head and his expression became more resolute, his voice flat but not unsympathetic. 'Your father did find the diamond pipe, Laura. As far as I'm concerned, you had the moral right to your share—his share really. Except we could never find him to give it to him. Not that we looked that hard. If Drew had wanted to find us . . . he knew where we were. But he never did. And we thought . . . let the past go. It seemed the only thing to do. But I wasn't expecting—how could I?—a daughter I didn't even know about.'

His thumb grazed softly down her cheek. 'You keep surprising me. I had you figured with no feelings at all. Except getting even. And now . . . perhaps I have to concede that I didn't quite get that right.'

Guilt squirmed inside Laura. Of course it had to have seemed that way to him . . . the way she'd gone about it . . . not knowing what hand she was playing until it was too late. 'I'm sorry if what I've done . . .'

'You're carrying your load, Laura,' he slid in softly. 'I carry mine.'

The unexpected empathy erased the inhibitions that had been crowding into her mind and the need which had brought her here once more clamoured for answers. 'Please . . . if you don't mind too much . . . would you tell me what my father was like, Jared?'

'From the viewpoint of a boy?'

'Yes. Anything.'

'He told us stories. He was always friendly. We liked him. I think you would have liked him too.'

She searched his eyes to see if he was lying, trying to make the best of the situation, then realised it didn't matter. 'Thank you,' she said huskily. 'It's very generous of you...telling me that. I appreciate it very much.'

'You're entitled,' he said gruffly. 'At least I had some years with my dad.'

His hand trailed from her cheek and he moved away from her. He took a few steps to the side of the baobab tree, then stood staring up at the mountains her father had painted. 'If it hadn't been for my mother, your father and mine could have been lifelong friends instead of rivals. They liked each other. It was the liking that made everything so much worse. Because it made the passions so much more intense. I understand all that now. I didn't then.'

The gravelled tone of his voice carried painful emotions and Laura moved instinctively to his side and touched his arm in tentative sympathy. 'I didn't mean to bring it all back to you, Jared.'

He looked down at her...and for a moment she saw mirrored in his eyes the same aching loneliness that she herself had known for so long. His arm lifted and curled around her shoulders, pulling her close to him. 'You came halfway around the world to see this sunset, Laura. Look now. It's starting.'

It felt good...deeply companionable...watching it together...sharing. For once there didn't seem to be any barriers between them...as much at one with each other as they were when they made love, but on a completely different plane. Maybe something new was starting between them. Laura fiercely hoped so.

As the sun slipped behind the mountains the sky came aflame like a burning sheet. Then, as that too sank, violet shadows crept over the land, and the reflection of the dying blaze turned the sky to frosted blues and pinks. It was an awesome panorama. Fire and ice. Passion and chilling aftermath. She could see why her father had painted it as he had. She hoped he was at peace now.

When Jared turned her back towards the camp, Laura was content to go, to finally put the past behind her and match her step with his wherever he led.

Johnno and Boodie had a fire going and dinner was well on the way to being cooked. They were delighted to show off their skills in front of Jared, and they grabbed the opportunity to ply him with questions about the muster. Laura listened to his replies, happy that he kept her at his side, his arm still curved around her. He didn't let her go until they sat down to eat what the boys had cooked.

A slow and eerie moonrise cast an entirely different light over the landscape...ghostly and full of dark phantoms. Laura was glad when the meal was over and Jared quietly invited her to share his sleeping-bag. And that was different too. Jared made no attempt to make love to her. He held her almost as though she were a child needing comfort.

'I'm glad you came,' she murmured. 'I didn't think you'd get back until tomorrow.'

'I'd finished all that I wanted to do and the men all reckoned that a new wife rated a higher priority than any help I could give them.' She could hear the smile in his voice. 'I was inclined to agree.'

She snuggled closer and he rubbed his cheek over her hair in a sweetly tender manner. 'You're not angry any more that I married you?' she asked.

'Something good might come of it yet.' It didn't sound as if he had too many doubts about that. In fact there was definitely a tone of smug satisfaction in his voice when he added, 'And if my recollection of the event is not entirely inaccurate, it was I who married you. I proposed. You accepted.'

'Only after suitable deliberation,' she countered, smiling to herself. 'I did measure you over for size with my eye first.'

'I measured up, then?' he asked, clearly amused by her contention.

'Fine,' she said. 'Just fine.'

His arm tightened around her then slowly relaxed. His hand ruffled gently through her hair. 'I'm glad I came out here tonight. To be with you. It's strange...but I feel at peace with everything...even myself.'

'Yes,' she sighed, feeling a wonderfully warm glow of satisfaction that it should be so.

He said no more and Laura didn't break the silence again either. Eventually she fell asleep to the soothing rhythm of his heartbeat.

CHAPTER TWELVE

JOHNNO and Boodie took Laura's horse back to the homestead, along with the message that the boss and his wife would fly in some time, after Miss Laura had been shown every square mile of Bendeneer Downs.

It was a tour that Laura hugged to her mind and heart and soul. 'Your place,' Jared had said just before they lifted away from the campsite, and the look in his eyes was more than an invitation to share it with him. It said that he wanted her to belong to it, as he did.

They followed the river that could dry up in drought seasons. They flew over the muster camps. Jared landed at some of the water-holes to show her the wildlife at close hand. The birds, particularly the flocks of cockatoos and the ibises, were fascinating. He took her all around the boundaries, pointed out the wild donkeys that had become a pest to graziers in the Kimberley, and the herds of cattle that would need mustering in the near future.

When they finally arrived home, they went into Harry's office to talk about what area they were going to fence off for the experimental breed of cattle. There was a detailed map of the whole station on the wall, and, while Laura had studied it before, it was far more real to her now that she could visualise all of its features. She listened to Jared and Harry discuss the pros and cons of various places, and although she ventured no opinion herself both men made her feel very much part of the discussion. They even looked to her for agreement when the decision was finally made.

All in all, Laura felt it was probably the happiest day of her life, and the new sense of togetherness that had been forged with Jared did not diminish in any way in the days that followed. It seemed to grow. They took time to understand each other, and their conversations were less and less guarded.

The men came home from the muster, and as was the custom—so Gwen told Laura—a day-long barbecue was held at the homestead. Huge sides of beef were turned on spits, potatoes cooked in the hot coals, salads, savoury dips, cakes and pies—it was one huge party that everyone thoroughly enjoyed.

Jared introduced Laura to all the stockmen and good-humouredly laughed at the somewhat ribald jokes directed his way. It was plain that they were happy to see him happy and they all welcomed Laura with open-hearted friendliness. After all, any woman who could rope and brand their boss had to be extra special.

And, much to Laura's intense pleasure, Jared not only gave them no argument on that score, but proved it over and over again in his manner to her. Gone was the indulgence of a dominant male to 'the little woman.' In its place was the easy camaraderie of partners who were attuned to each other. Pride there certainly was, just as she was proud to own him as her husband. And as far as any physical expression of their relationship was concerned, Jared had no compunction whatsoever about demonstrating that he enjoyed having her close to him, whether it was simply a hand at her waist or a hug around the shoulders.

As the day wore into evening, musical instruments were brought out: guitars, piano accordians and mouth organs which several of the stockmen could play with incredible skill. Everyone gathered around for a sing-along of favourite old tunes—'Roll out the Barrel', and many more of that ilk. One of the stockmen, an expatriate

Scot, donned his kilt and did a highland dance to a piano accordian rendition of 'Scotland the Brave'. Then some of Charlie Biraban's people played the didgeridoo, while a group of boys did a hunting dance. It was simple entertainment, but Laura couldn't remember having enjoyed an evening more, and as she walked back up to the big house with Jared she thought the world of more sophisticated culture well lost for the world of Bendeneer Downs.

Jared started giving her lessons on the technicalities of flying helicopters. The new fencing got into full swing. Laura was inveigled into giving the schoolchildren a talk about Zimbabwe and the way of life there. They enjoyed it so much that Jill suggested she give more 'People and Society' talks about all the other countries that Laura had first-hand knowledge about. It was more story-time than a formal lesson and it soon became a regular fixture in the school routine, much to everyone's pleasure. Apart from these recollections for the children's benefit, Laura had virtually dismissed the outside world from her mind when the call from her mother came. She and Jared had just finished breakfast one morning and were about to set out to inspect the progress of the fencing when Harry called out from his office.

. 'Laura...an international radio-call for you. From Boston.'

'My mother. Probably about what clothes to send me. Or some more questions about you,' she tossed at Jared as she hurried along the veranda. 'Wait for me.'

'Maybe I'd better monitor your answers,' he said teasingly, and strolled after her.

But Laura was wrong on both counts. And Connie Hammond was very decisive about what she wanted.

'Laura, I've booked a flight to Sydney. It gets in early Sunday morning. Ted has arranged for a limousine to pick me up at the airport and take me to the Sheraton-

Wentworth Hotel. I'll spend a day there to recover from the trip. I want to know how to get to Bendeneer Downs after that.'

Laura was so astonished that her mother would even contemplate coming to visit her on the cattle station that she was lost for words. Jared, who had heard the message, took over the call.

'Mrs Hammond, this is Jared Eastern. I'll have one of my people contact you at the Sheraton to make whatever arrangements suit you on the Monday. My Lear Jet will be standing by to fly you here. It is simply a matter of your convenience.'

'Oh! Thank you. That's...that's very kind of you, Jared.' She sounded flustered by the generosity inherent in Jared's self-introduction.

'Not at all. We will look forward to making you welcome here at Bendeneer Downs. I'll pass you back to Laura now.'

Laura still hadn't recovered her composure. 'Mom? Did you get my letter?' Perhaps it hadn't arrived yet and her mother didn't know what she was coming to.

'Yes, dear. And the photographs. I've never seen you look so... They're beautiful, Laura.' There was a slight catch in her voice, then more briskly, 'I've packed up all the things you want and I'll bring them with me.'

'Thank you,' Laura managed weakly. If her mother had received the letter she could have no illusions about what to expect. 'It's...it's good of you to come...such a long way.'

'I want to see where you've finally settled down, Laura. It sounds...very interesting. And, of course, I want to meet your husband.'

'Of course,' Laura echoed, then finally pulled herself together. 'We'll look forward to seeing you, Mom.'

'Thank Jared again for me. Goodbye now, dear.'

It was only after the call ended that the full ramifications of her mother's visit hit Laura. She shot Jared a look of urgent appeal as they left the office. 'Jared, there are some things I have to tell you. Some things I have to explain.'

Jared raised a quizzical eyebrow. 'I doubt there's anything your mother can throw at me that I can't handle, Laura.'

'It's not that. She's far too polite to say anything critical to you. Although she has an...an ingrained snobbery and...and social-mindedness that will probably test your patience. But it won't be a long visit. This isn't her kind of world. If you know Boston society at all——'

'Laura, she either accepts us and the way we want to live, or she doesn't,' Jared said firmly. 'I will extend every courtesy to your mother. How she reacts to Bendeneer Downs is her business. I hope it's in a favourable way. If not, she can leave whenever she wishes. Her visit is no problem to me.' His eyes were sharply watchful as he added, 'I didn't marry your mother. Now what's the problem to you?'

'My mother doesn't know anything about my father's connection to this place. Or to your family. Or to the diamond mine. Only about the paintings. So...' Laura gestured her dilemma '...there's no point in mentioning anything about the past.'

'Better for it not to be brought up at all. If your mother ever mentions Drew——'

'That's not likely,' Laura put in sharply. 'My father has always been very much a skeleton in my mother's closet.'

Jared eyed her curiously. 'Like to tell me why?'

Laura's mouth twisted in bitter irony. 'He was a mistake. I was a mistake. They married because of me. It was the respectable thing to do.'

She dragged in a deep breath and tried to shrug off the negative image. 'Don't get me wrong, Jared. My mother always did her best for me. We just don't think the same way. But she is my mother. And I'm her daughter. And I'm glad she's making the effort to come, even though we don't get on well at close quarters.'

Jared drew her into a gentle embrace. A twinkle of amusement overlaid something else in his eyes, something that made Laura's heart lurch. 'How did a savage pagan witch like you cover her true colours in Boston society?' he asked.

'It's a long story,' she replied, striving for lightness to cover the mad leap of her pulse.

'You must tell me some time,' he murmured, and kissed her with a slow sensuality that somehow imparted more tenderness than desire. When he lifted his head, his eyes held no amusement at all. They held a look that seemed both possessive and protective.

'Don't ever think of yourself as a mistake again,' he commanded, softly but very firmly. 'You're no mistake, Laura. Not to me or anyone on Bendeneer Downs. And this is *your place*. You keep that in mind...' his lips twitched into a smile '...partner!'

She almost said it—*I love you, Jared*. She barely caught the words back. And for a long time afterwards Laura wondered how Jared would react if she did say them. She had thought, for a moment, just before he had kissed her, that he might have come to love her. But it was extremely doubtful that he would ever admit any vulnerability to a woman. Even if he did feel it.

Laura once again resigned herself to being content with their relationship just the way it was. After all, she now had everything she wanted. She didn't need to have it labelled 'love'. Certainly her mother wouldn't find any fault in Jared's manner towards her daughter. They were partners and lovers. And no one could hope for much more than that in a marriage.

The week before her mother's visit raced by. When the jet flew in on Monday afternoon, Laura and Jared were at the airstrip in the Jeep, ready to meet and transport their visitor to the big house. All the homestead children were either sitting or dangling over the stockyard fence, eager to see Miss Laura's mother from the American city of Boston, which had been pointed out to them on a map of the USA.

Connie Hammond didn't disappoint them. She emerged from the jet looking like a fashion model on safari. The elegant white trouser-suit had a long flowing coat. She wore a white straw hat with a stylish brim, and around its crown was tied a long silk scarf in a black and white zebra print, which matched the shirt under the coat. Her lovely face was beautifully made up, her nails perfectly manicured, and she looked all class, right down to the black and white walking shoes.

The children instantly started waving to her, and after a moment's hesitation, and much to Laura's relief, Connie Hammond lifted her hand and gave them a royal wave back. But her smile to Laura and Jared looked stiff and a little uncertain as she came down the steps from the plane. She seemed to relax a little when Laura gave her a hug and kissed her on the cheek.

'It's lovely to see you, Mother,' she said as warmly as she could, then turned to her husband and proudly linked her arm around his. 'And this, of course, is Jared.'

'Welcome to Bendeneer Downs, Mrs Hammond,' Jared said with a flashing white smile that was aimed to charm.

Connie Hammond stared up at him for several long seconds before she recollected herself and took the hand offered to her. 'Forgive me,' she said, flushing in painful embarrassment at her lapse in manners. 'You just reminded me so strongly of...of someone else. Not in looks but...Oh, my! I am making such a hash of this. And I'm very pleased to meet you, Jared. And do call me Connie,' she finished in an anxious rush.

This was so unlike her mother's usual polished composure that Laura could hardly keep her surprise from showing. And it was only the first surprise of many. Not one word of criticism—about anything—passed Connie Hammond's lips. The big house was 'most impressive'; the room Laura gave her 'most lovely'; Gwen and Harry were 'the nicest people'.

When Jared informed her during the course of dinner that they were preparing for a shipment of cattle—an experimental breed that Laura had suggested—Connie Hammond beamed proudly at her daughter. 'Well, you mustn't let me take up any of your time. Both of you go right ahead with whatever needs doing. I'm so fascinated by all that Laura wrote me about the life here that I'll be very happy just pottering around the homestead.'

Jared took her at her word, but Laura couldn't believe it at first. However, the next day her mother went out of her way to make the acquaintance of everyone at the station, and not once did she emit the slightest hint of snobbishness or prejudice. She even found Johnno and Boodie 'charming boys', and said she would certainly take up their offer to go riding with them so they could show her everything like they did with Miss Laura.

'You don't have to stay with me, dear,' she gently admonished Laura. 'You go along with Jared. Gwen said I could ask her anything. And Harry's going to explain how the working year is organised on a cattle station. So you don't have to worry about me.'

As astonished as Laura was by her mother's attitude, she was also intensely gratified by it. It demonstrated the kind of acceptance that she had always wanted from her mother, and certainly generated a very relaxed atmosphere that she had never enjoyed in her mother's presence before. For the first time in her life, Laura wasn't made to feel that something more was expected of her.

'It must be you,' she told Jared that night. 'She took one look at you and decided you were a man she'd better not tangle with.'

'Mmm...most unlike her daughter,' he commented smugly, running a teasing caress along her thigh which was pleasurably entangled with his.

She laughed. 'You were begging to be tangled with, Jared. You were so terribly arrogant. And sexy.'

'Well, if all I am to you is a body...'

He proceeded to use it in a way that obliterated any further thoughts about her mother.

The day before the cattle were to arrive, Jared took them both on a tour of the diamond mine. He presented Connie with a magnificent multicoloured diamond which she could have set any way she liked. Laura was deeply touched when her mother's eyes filled with emotional tears and the words she spoke were so unmistakably from the heart.

'Thank you, Jared. I'll always treasure it. But I'd like to say that you've already given me the best thing. To see Laura so happy with you means more to me than anything else. I was so afraid...' She smiled at Laura through her tears. 'But it's all right. I thought you'd never find what you were looking for. But I can see you have. And I know you won't let go.'

She turned a rueful look back at Jared. 'She's like that, you know.'

'Yes. I know,' Jared answered drily, and moved to hug Laura close to him. He smiled down at her. 'Utterly ruthless, this daughter of yours, Connie. Once she gets her teeth into something, there's no stopping her. She uses me quite shamelessly to get what she wants...'

Connie laughed. 'I haven't noticed you looking dissatisfied with that, Jared.'

'She's a witch, Connie. She cast a spell on me.'

And instead of denying what he said, or even correcting him in any way, Laura laughed with her mother, revelling in her mother's pleasure, marvelling that underneath the disapproval of all those years there had been a very deep and constant caring for her. It was only afterwards that Laura wondered if Jared really did think she was using him to get what she wanted. It was an uncomfortable thought and she dismissed it. After all, they were happy together.

They were both in particularly high spirits the next afternoon when the freight-plane from the Cocos Islands touched down at Bendeneer Downs. Everyone at the homestead was down near the airstrip to see the new breed of cattle arrive. The stockmen were there on their horses, ready to direct the small herd into a nearby stockyard where they would be fed and watered and settled down after their long trip. Laura and Jared were standing by the Jeep, eagerly awaiting first sight of their investment in this experimental project.

A ramp was fitted up against the plane and finally the door was opened. One by one the cattle came streaming out, snorting and bucking a little with the excitement of being released from close confinement. The stockmen moved in to control any straying from the direction they wanted the herd to take. Laura's view was obscured by one of the horses and she moved a few steps away from the Jeep. Whether her movement caught the attention of the young bull as it came off the ramp, she was never to know. The animal pawed the ground, sized her up, and charged with crazed disregard for anything else around it.

Then everything happened so fast that there were only frames of horrified images left in her mind. Jared screaming her name, leaping in front of her, grabbing at the bull's horns, being gored and tossed in the air, trampled on, a horn ripping down his face, what sounded like a cannon-shot, the bull toppling slowly on top of him, and Jared... Jared lying still... bleeding... so still... her own voice screaming his name... arms holding her back as the men closed in on him, lifted the bull away, and Jared not moving... not moving at all.

She broke free of the arms trying to restrain her. She was running, stumbling, tearing off her shirt to staunch the bleeding, crying out, 'Jared... Jared... Jared...'

He wasn't dead. He was still breathing. But no one attempted to move him. Laura sat on the dirt beside him and gently dabbed her shirt at the terrible gashes on his face. Then Gwen was kneeling beside her, taking the cloth from her, doing a more efficient job of stopping up the blood. Laura stroked Jared's hand, desperately willing him to live. She didn't know how long they'd been there when his fingers slowly flexed under hers.

'Laura...' It was the barest of whispers. He didn't open his eyes, but a line creased between his brows as if he was struggling towards consciousness.

'I'm here, Jared. I'm here,' she cried.

'Don't...' She bent closer to his lips to catch whatever he was trying to say. 'It's no use... I'm badly hurt... let me die...'

'No! I won't let you,' she insisted passionately. 'I need you, Jared. I won't let you die. I love you. I love you.'

His eyes flickered half open and pain looked out of them... agonising pain. 'Can't live... in cage...'

Her soul twisted with the knowledge of what he meant. He would rather be dead than caged in a body that wouldn't do what he wanted of it. He would set all the wild animals free. He shot cattle that were too weak to survive by themselves. An act of mercy.

'No...' she moaned. 'No...'

'Your place . . . yours now . . .'

'I don't want it. Not without you. Jared . . . Jared . . .'

Harry was at his side. A hypodermic syringe was inserted into his arm. Another. Shooting him full of emergency morphine.

'I love you, Jared,' Laura pleaded. There seemed to be a slight flicker of recognition in his dulling eyes. 'I'm carrying your child. You've *got* to live.'

The lids dropped shut as if they were too heavy to hold open. Laura didn't think he had heard the last bit, the most important bit that she had been holding back from telling him until the matter was totally beyond doubt. But she was sure in her own mind. And he had to know about it now. Had to. 'Your child, Jared,' she repeated with desperate vehemence, hoping to reach into his mind.

But there were no more words from him. He had slipped back into unconsciousness. A stretcher was brought and Jared was carefully lifted on to it. Towels were put around his wounds to check the bleeding. Then the Lear Jet was screaming in from the mine, taxiing to a halt; Harry yelling instructions as the men carried Jared to the plane; her mother accompanying her as she followed the stretcher on which Jared lay so still, so . . . They had to get him to a hospital, and as quickly as possible. Kununura, Harry said, five hundred miles away.

Her love for Jared was a leaden weight on her heart. Did it mean anything? Would he fight to live now? If he had heard about the child, he surely would. That had to mean something to him . . . his very own flesh and blood . . . a son or a daughter who needed a father. It had to make his life worth having, even if it wasn't quite the life he had enjoyed before.

Jared had told her he would never fight for her. He had also said he would never die for her. Yet when the moment had come, he had thrown his life away to save hers. Perhaps he loved her. And he thought she only wanted his body and the place he could give her. Maybe it wasn't only despair over being left caged. If he felt he couldn't be what she wanted any more...sexy... irresistible...better than any other men. The recollections streamed across her mind...the night he had made her tell him he was more than any other man...other, more flippant remarks that might have held his innermost beliefs.

The Lear Jet took off. One hour. Live for one hour, Jared. Please, my love...until we get help.

The painful treadmill of her thoughts went on and on as they flew towards Kununura. Her only consolation was that she didn't have to make a decision yet. After they got to a hospital, after the doctors had examined him properly...when the options were made clear...

But she also saw Jared's need. Even if they could mend his body and give it back to him in good working order, she, who had lived with disfigurement for so long, understood it better than anyone else. Superficial attraction—surface looks—wasn't a factor in her relationship or understanding of other people. Not any more. She couldn't remember if she'd told Jared that or not, but if he lived, she had to make him believe that truth. He would have to undergo the trial of strength that she had borne so many years ago. She would help him as best she could, aided by her own experience.

She turned to Harry, who kept vigil with her. 'Tell the pilot to radio ahead that we need the best plastic surgeon in the country. Get them to find him. Get him there,' she ordered.

And as he left her to carry out her command, she gave another silent command to the man who was her life. 'Love me, Jared. Love me enough to want to live.'

CHAPTER THIRTEEN

JARED was strong enough, Laura kept arguing to herself. If anyone could pull through the shock and trauma of the surgery, he could. On a purely physical basis, those doctors had the fittest, healthiest body they could possibly have to help them succeed in their task. But the will to live...did Jared have that? Did he want her badly enough?

At Kununura they had given him massive blood transfusions and put him on a life-support system. His pulse was weak and erratic, his blood pressure too low. After consultations it was decided that it was in Jared's best interests to transfer him to the teaching hospital in Adelaide.

How many hours had it been now? Eight? Nine? The flight to Kununura...the emergency treatment that ensured Jared remained in a stable enough condition for the flight over the centre of Australia to the city of Adelaide...to this huge hospital...the X-rays...papers to sign that committed Jared into the hands of the surgeons—papers he might not have signed himself—but she had made the decision. Whether he wanted it or not, she would do everything possible to keep him alive.

'Coffee, Laura.'

She looked up at her mother who had quietly kept her company all these hours, unobtrusively doing things for her. The shirt and jacket she wore were what her mother had handed to her. The uneaten sandwiches that had been produced from nowhere. Even soup that had somehow been inveigled from a staff kitchen. She suddenly realised that she had barely acknowledged these things.

'I'm sorry I haven't thanked you...' She shook her head as tears swam into her eyes.

Her mother gently squeezed her shoulder. 'I don't expect you to talk, Laura,' she said softly. 'You never did...not when things were hard for you.'

'I don't mean to shut you out, Mom. But I can't express what I feel...'

'I know, dear.' Connie Hammond heaved a deep sigh. 'Don't think I don't see my own mistakes, Laura. It's too late to change them now, but...there are some things I'd like to tell you...things I've kept shut up inside myself all these years...and they might help you feel...less lonely.'

'That's kind of you,' Laura assented, touched by the sympathetic understanding in her mother's eyes.

A sad little smile curved her mouth. 'You're very like your father, Laura. You have his eyes. And even as a child, you looked at me as he did.' The smile turned down into a rueful grimace. 'I tried so hard to forget him. But you never let me. Even to some of the things you said...so like Drew...and I had to keep fighting them, or the choice I'd made would have been unbearable.'

Laura shook her head. 'Mom, you don't have to explain to me what went wrong between you and my father.'

'I think you should know, Laura. There was no man before or since that ever quite measured up to Drew. He was...he was like Jared. When I stepped off the plane at Bendeneer Downs that first afternoon...my heart turned over. Jared has exactly that same air of..."there's a world out there to conquer and I'm the one to conquer it".'

She paused, her eyes softening with memories. Laura remembered the odd loss of composure that had struck her at the time. If her father had exuded that same quality... yes, she could see how Jared could claim that her father and his might have been lifelong friends, if they hadn't been destined to be rivals... over a woman. That superior challenging air... would Jared still retain it after his injuries?

'When you wrote and told me where Bendeneer Downs was... I had to come,' her mother continued, dragging Laura's attention back to her.

All these years with not a word about her father...she had to listen... to understand what her mother was saying. Such a confidence might never come again. Only in moments of crisis did people dismiss everything else but the truth. She had to listen... concentrate... take in what her mother was confiding to her...

'I told myself it was to see you and Jared, but... The Kimberley was where your father was heading... where he wanted me to come with him... to find what could be found. I'd never heard of such a place. And Australia...so far away... I wouldn't leave Boston. And Drew wouldn't stay. He wouldn't even try to fit in. He scorned the life that was the only life I knew...too narrow and confined, too fully of silly rules and conventions that had no meaning for him...'

She shook her head and her eyes refocused on Laura's in painful self-mockery. 'I didn't understand until I came. Didn't realise how vast... and daunting this country is. Not until I flew over it. Once I saw it all— the mine, the cattle station—I knew why Drew couldn't be content in Boston. I finally knew. And I see how right it is for you and Jared. And I wonder if...'

Her mouth twisted into a grimace. 'But I didn't have the courage to take on a world I didn't know. It wasn't important enough to me, Laura. To be... Drew's partner...no matter what. I made my choice. And I set about justifying it in every way I could...marrying Ted...making all the *right* connections, doing all the *right* things...and I wanted you to do the same, Laura. To be like me because...because that would have made me even more right...'

An obsession...rooted in the pain of a love that hadn't met her preconceived expectations. No wonder she had refused to speak about Andrew McKenzie. It hurt too much, Laura realised, and with understanding came a ready forgiveness for all her mother's driven need to be successful in her chosen world.

'I've always been a disappointment to you——'

'No...no...this is right for you!' her mother said vehemently. 'I understand now...don't you see? I hated Drew for not doing what I wanted...and I was frustrated with you for turning your back on the life I felt I was building for you. Your father all over again...rejecting what I valued. You'd have that look of distance in your eyes, as if you were seeing another world altogether...and finally I wanted to see it too. And I have. I'll never feel the same way about it again. Even your father...I can forgive him now. He was big enough. I wasn't.'

Who knows what drives any other human being? Laura thought with deep humility. Who can judge...anyone? She looked at her mother, feeling a depth of compassion she had never felt before for the woman who had lived her own private hell, doing her best, trying to achieve something that would prove her life worthwhile.

'Mom, you're not unhappy with Ted, are you? I always thought...'

'That we were two of a kind. And we are, dear. He's an ornament to my life, and I'm an ornament to his,' she said drily. 'We understand each other, and that's comfortable. But we never had what you and Jared have...what I had very briefly with your father. And I'm glad you have that, Laura. In my heart, despite all the conflict between us, I truly did always want the best for you.'

Laura reached out and squeezed her hand. 'I do know that, Mom. But thanks for telling me. And for telling me all the rest. For what it's worth, you probably made the right decision to stay in Boston, even though the parting with my father hurt so badly. I know that Jared's mother hated living in the Kimberley...the isolation...the lack of civilised comforts and company. After Jared's father died, she married a man who could give her what Ted gives you. So...who knows what was right or wrong? One of the first things Jared said to me was...let the past go. It doesn't matter, Mom. What matters is now. And tomorrow. And...'

If Jared died...what tomorrow would there be for her? She shut her eyes tight against the tears that threatened. She would not be weak. She had to be strong. She had to make him want to live.

'Laura...I just wanted you to know that...that I'm here for you. That I'm not...without some understanding. If you'd like to talk...if it would help pass the time...'

The pained offer beat at Laura's heart. Her mother had bared her soul for her sake. Not to respond would be like another rejection...yet she wasn't used to sharing her innermost thoughts and feelings. It didn't come easy. But when had anything worthwhile been easy? If only she had told Jared she loved him before...

'I'm scared, Mom,' she blurted out. 'I'm so terribly scared that I won't be enough for Jared. He doesn't want to be caged inside a body that...that...that isn't perfect.'

'Laura, it may not come to that. There's hope, dear. There's always hope.'

'He might hate me——'

'No! Don't think that. Don't ever think that, Laura. Jared knew what he was doing. I saw it all. The look on his face just before he leapt to take the bull's charge away from you. It wasn't an impulsive, instinctive thing. His fear...horror...of losing you...was so naked... anything was preferable. Even dying.'

Laura forced her eyes open to search her mother's face, unconvinced but wanting desperately to believe. 'It won't make any difference to me if he's crippled or disfigured. I'll love him just the same,' she declared with vehement passion.

'I know you will, Laura,' came the soft reply. 'And you'll find a way to make Jared believe that. If you have to. You are the one person who can do that, Laura.'

'Am I, Mom?' Uncertainty wobbled through her voice.

Her mother smiled and tenderly stroked the hair back from her temples. 'When have you ever been beaten, Laura? Even when you had so much to suffer yourself, you defied the world to think the less of you. And scorned those who did...including me. But I promise you, I won't make that same mistake again. Whatever happens, Laura, you can count on whatever support you want from me.'

The tears she had tried to suppress swam into her eyes. 'Thank you,' she whispered huskily, then hugged her mother with a fullness of heart she had never felt with her before. 'I thought I'd never measure up to what you wanted.'

'My dear, you're what I wish I could have been,' her mother said wistfully. 'Remember that when I do fail you in any way. And don't hesitate to tell me what I'm doing wrong.'

Laura pulled back and managed a shaky smile. 'I'm hardly perfect myself. But I won't retreat from you again, Mom. I promise.'

The sound of footsteps approaching along the hospital corridor had Laura whirling to her feet. Her pulse starting drumming, her mind jagging between fear and hope. But the two people who turned the corner into the waiting-room were not doctors or nurses with news of Jared. They were Naomi and Rafe Carellan.

It was Rafe who broke the awkward silence. 'We got here as soon as we could, Laura. Mrs Hammond...I'm Rafe Carellan and this is my wife, Naomi. Jared's mother.'

'Connie... Connie Hammond.' She took the hand offered. 'I'm sorry we're meeting in such circumstances.'

Naomi Carellan didn't even look at her. She was staring at Laura with wildly accusing eyes. 'You did this, didn't you? If you hadn't been there——'

'Naomi! Stop it!' Rafe hissed at her, his eyes stabbing a begging plea at Laura. 'She doesn't mean that.'

Naomi was too worked up, too distraught to listen to him. 'I knew something dreadful would happen. It was all a lie, wasn't it? You were after——'

'Don't you put your sense of guilt on me, Mrs Carellan,' Laura cut in, her voice shaking from her own pent-up inner agony. 'This accident wasn't caused by any human failings.'

Naomi Carellan didn't even pause to take that in. The bitterly accusing words kept spilling from her lips. 'I knew it would come to no good. I knew it would never work. You fooled him just to——'

Laura's control completely snapped. The exhaustive tension she had been under exploded into a passionate outpouring that finally silenced the woman.

'Who do you think you are?' she railed at Naomi. 'The world does not revolve around you, Mrs Carellan. Jared is all the world I want. And don't you dare taint it with yours. I don't care about your damned diamond

mine. I don't care about what you did in the past except
in so far as it affected Jared. You're so wrapped up in
yourself you never even saw his loneliness. His needs.
Only yours ever counted——'

'Laura!' It was a hoarse protest from Rafe but it didn't
stop her.

'Do what you want with your life, but I'm not going
to let you poison Jared's and mine!' she flung at them
both. 'Just get out of here! Go back home! Jared doesn't
belong to you any more. Even if he ever did. Which I
doubt. He's my husband now and I love him. I'd give
my life for his if I could. I wish it were me in there on
the operating-table. And so help me God, if either of
you ever says or does anything that will make Jared not
want to live, I'll...'

A huge lump swelled into her throat. Tears spurted
into her eyes. She flapped her hands helplessly, then
suddenly found herself taken forcefully into her mother's
arms and cuddled like a child.

'I don't know what's going on here,' Connie
Hammond stated curtly. 'But Laura has been under
enormous strain. If either of you has any doubt that my
daughter would marry Jared for any other reason than
that she loved him, I can assure you, there are quite a
few very wealthy men in Boston who——'

'Mrs Hammond...' Rafe cut in urgently, then in a
tone of despairing impatience, 'Naomi, for God's sake!
For your son's sake, snap out of this! What more do
you have to hear or see? What you're doing is destructive. It always has been destructive! You eat people
up until they're so screwed around——'

'Rafe?' Naomi's voice quavered at the removal of the
support she had depended on for so long.

'Face it, Naomi! For once in your life, face what
you're doing and stop it!' he pleaded hoarsely. 'Jared
loves Laura. Laura loves Jared. It has nothing to do

with you or me or anyone else. Only them! And you're just making everything worse than it already is.'

'But you know——'

'I only know that I'm tired of it, Naomi,' came the flat, weary retort. 'Deadly tired. I'm going to sit here quietly and wait with Laura and her mother. And if there's anything I can do for Jared or Laura, I'll do it. You do what you like. I don't care. I just don't care any more.'

'Rafe, I... I'm sorry...'

'It's not good enough being sorry!' he rasped. 'If you can't be kind, then go. It's one or the other. Is that clear? How can I make it any clearer? All I can think of is that just for once you might think of someone else besides yourself!'

He took a few paces forward. His strong hand clamped down on Laura's shoulder. 'Is there anything I can do, Laura?'

She shook her head, too distressed to speak.

'Mrs Hammond, there is no excuse I can give for my wife's behaviour,' Rafe stated bleakly. 'I hope you can both bear with me. With us... if my wife chooses to stay. Jared is as much a son to me as if he were my own flesh and blood. And...'

'Of course you must stay, Mr Carellan. And you also, Mrs Carellan,' Connie Hammond said with quiet dignity. 'I think, perhaps, it's times like these that bring out the best, and the worst in us. Shall we forget this... this unfortunate scene... and just pray that Jared gets well?'

Laura had no idea how much longer it was that they waited for news. Not another word passed Naomi's lips. From time to time Rafe spoke to her mother and her mother replied something. She herself felt too drained and numb to do anything but withdraw inside herself and keep willing Jared to live. When finally there were more footsteps along the corridor, Laura could barely stumble to her feet. The head surgeon swept into the waiting-room accompanied by a nurse.

'Ah... Mrs Eastern. Your husband is doing as well as can be expected...'

Laura sagged a little and her mother's arm went around her waist, holding tightly.

'He'll be in intensive care for some time, but his condition is stable...'

'His... his legs?' Laura whispered.

The surgeon smiled. 'Well, he won't be leaping around in a hurry with a broken pelvis, but the paralysis was caused by a pinched nerve which we have relieved. I foresee no permanent damage on that count. The two broken ribs did not pierce anything vital. We were lucky there. His face will require further work at a later date, but for the present we've done a fair job of stitching him all back together. Needless to say, he is not a pretty sight at the moment, but, I trust, slightly better than when you brought him in. And providing his strong constitution does its work——'

'Can I see him now? Be with him?' Laura asked anxiously, fearful that Jared's mind might overrule his constitution if she weren't there to assure him that life would be worth living.

'I don't see why not,' the surgeon replied kindly. 'Sister will take you to his room. But you do appreciate, Mrs Eastern, that he won't regain consciousness for some hours. In fact, he'll be under sedation for a few days.'

'I've got to stay with him,' Laura stated determinedly.

The surgeon considered her for a moment then nodded. 'Sister, arrange a bed for Mrs Eastern in Mr Eastern's room.'

'I'll bring you some things in the morning, Laura,' her mother said quickly.

'And I'll see your mother to a hotel,' Rafe added.

'Laura…' Naomi clutched at her hand. Her eyes were dark pools of turbulent emotion. Then suddenly she shook her head and dropped her grasp. 'Go…go to him. Give him what I can't.'

Naomi's acceptance of her barely impinged on Laura's mind. Nothing else mattered but to get to Jared's side without another second's delay. If he regained consciousness only fleetingly, she had to be there. He had to be assured that she would always be there for him. She would never let him go. She would take his hand and hold it, so he was aware that she was there, even if he was unable to open his eyes. And talk to him. Tell him all the things they were going to do together…share together…

The long vigil had begun.

CHAPTER FOURTEEN

THE first time Jared regained consciousness, he wasn't exactly lucid. 'Hardest game of football I've ever played,' he mumbled to no one in particular. He looked at Laura without any recognition at all. 'Did we beat them?'

'Yes. We won,' she said, instinctively emphasising the positive.

'Serve 'em right,' he agreed, his eyes dulling as the lids dropped shut again.

Disorientation was only to be expected, the nurse informed Laura, particularly when coming out of anaesthetic. His brains weren't scrambled. There was nothing to worry about. More likely than not, the last time Mr Eastern had been taken to hospital was for an injury from a game of football. Quite often a patient's mind would naturally block out the trauma of an accident for days afterwards, like a defence mechanism against something unacceptable.

Laura relaxed a little, but the nurse's advice made her even more conscious of the necessity to reassure Jared before his mind grasped *the unacceptable*. She kept talking softly to him but had no idea if he heard anything of what she said. In the end, sheer exhaustion took its toll, and she rested her head beside the hand she was holding.

The painful pressure on her fingers woke her. Jared's hand was clutching hers with convulsive strength. His eyes were tightly closed, his mouth a thin line. Either mental or physical agony was pouring through the fingers crushing hers. Laura ignored the pain. She didn't care if he broke her bones if it helped him. She talked as fast as she could.

'Jared, the cage is only temporary. You'll emerge from it fit and whole, I promise you. Just hang on, my darling. It's going to take time for you to mend, but you can do it. It's only a matter of time before you'll be on your feet again, doing whatever you want. You won't be incapacitated in any way. So please, my love, you have to live through this. I need you, Jared. But even more importantly, our child needs you. You can't let anything stop you from having what you always wanted. You're not alone any more. You'll never be alone again...'

His fingers gradually relaxed, fretted briefly at hers, then fell into limpness again. Laura heaved a deep sigh and gently lifted his hand to her cheek, needing to recapture the feeling of being wanted by him. She trailed his fingers down her skin as he had so often done, and when she once more rested her head beside him, she kept his hand cradled at her face.

When next she woke it was to a light feathering touch that brushed across her temples. 'Jared?' she whispered, not sure if he was awake or merely restive.

'You're real?'

The strained murmur jerked her head up. His eyes were barely opened slits, but the dull pain in them sharpened to something else when he saw her...a searching need for answers.

'You've been with me? Talking to me?' he asked.

'Yes...yes,' she answered huskily, almost choked by a tidal wave of emotion.

'I thought...a dream.'

'Not a dream, Jared,' she assured him, clasping his hand with both of hers to impress him with her reality. 'Everything I said was true,' she added with all the passionate conviction in her heart.

'Did you say...did you speak of a child, Laura?'

'Yes. We're going to have one, Jared. In about eight months' time. And then I'll need you to sit with me because I don't know how to have a baby and you'll have to hold my hand and——'

'And not let go,' he said with a ghost of a smile.

'Never let go,' she insisted fiercely.

His eyelids dropped shut, but the faint smile lingered on his lips for several moments before it faded away. At last Laura could rest content, assured that Jared wouldn't let his life slip away, not if he could help it. Secure in the knowledge that it was now safe to leave his side, Laura allowed herself to be persuaded into using the bed that had been provided for her.

She slept deeply and long, her own body insisting on having its energy level renewed. For almost twenty hours she heard nothing of the coming and going of doctors, or anything else. When she finally opened her eyes it was to see her mother sitting beside her.

'It's all right, dear. Jared's doing fine,' she said quietly.

Laura bolted upright to make certain it was so. Jared was still in the room with her, swathed in bandages, the lower half of his body held in a traction unit.

'The doctors are very satisfied with his progress,' her mother continued quickly. 'No sign of infection from his wounds and everything on the way to healing as it should.'

'Thanks, Mom.'

'Now what you need is a long, hot shower, a change of clean clothes, and a hearty meal,' her mother said sternly. 'No argument, Laura. You've got to keep your strength up. I'll stay here with Jared in case he wakes and asks about you.'

'Has he done that while I was asleep?' Laura asked anxiously.

'No cause for you to worry.' Connie Hammond gave her a dry smile. 'All he wants to know is that you're all right. Anyone would think there was nothing else he cared about.'

Laura's heart immediately lightened and she hugged her mother, feeling too emotional to express herself in words. Connie Hammond patted her daughter's back. 'Go on now. Make yourself look good for your husband.'

Laura smiled at her mother's philosophy of life, but she didn't criticise it. Not this time. Looking good might be a superficial thing but it had its place, and Laura was willing to do anything that might make Jared feel better. He was awake when she returned fully refreshed, and Connie Hammond tactfully left them alone together.

'A month of this, I'm told,' Jared said, his voice a rasp of resignation.

'Something like that,' Laura agreed, her eyes holding his with firm resolution, knowing that if he had been told that much he would have insisted on being told the rest.

'You know I'm going to look a mess, Laura.'

'In the short term, yes,' she said unequivocally, hearing the note of uncertainty in his voice and steadfastly dismissing any need for it. 'But they can do wonders with cosmetic surgery these days, Jared. In any case, the scars don't matter unless you let them eat into your mind. I know. I've had them.'

His mouth twisted. 'I was thinking more about how they were going to affect you. Difficult for a wife who has a husband she wants to hide.'

'Is that all you are, Jared? A face?' she challenged, attacking the wall he would build between them before it got cemented into place. 'Do you think that's all you are to me?'

He didn't answer straight away. Laura could sense his tension, but it was important that he assess what she was saying, to measure the weight of truth and not allow superficial assumptions to cloud his judgement. So she didn't rush into explaining her own experience.

'Laura, one thing I'm not . . . is a fool,' he said with deadly seriousness. 'And one thing I am . . . is a realist. I still have my life. That's a plus. There are things I'd like to do with it. Being a father to our child is one of them. For that . . . I will always be grateful to you.'

His voice hardened as he continued, spelling out the reality of his experience. 'But I know that changes generate other changes. Cause and effect. And, with all the will in the world, there are some reactions that cannot be controlled. To be frank with you, I'd rather remember what we had than——'

'Than see me wince away from the sight of you, Jared?' she supplied softly, understanding all too well what he meant.

'Something like that,' he said tightly.

Irony lent a slight curl to her mouth as she answered him. 'Remember that morning we met for breakfast to discuss my father's painting . . . you lumped me in with all the very beautiful women who thought diamonds were their best friends. You didn't know me then. There are things you still don't know about me, Jared. You see, I don't think of myself as beautiful. I'm the person who lives behind this face, no matter what it looks like. I made up my mind to that a long time ago, when even my mother would wince away at the sight of me.'

'From you? But why?'

'Because I was a mess,' Laura replied matter-of-factly. 'All through my adolescent years there was nothing anyone could do for me. I endured a hormonal imbalance that made my face—at best—a social joke. Even when my body chemistry corrected itself I was left with scars that were eventually erased by a special laser treatment.'

She picked up his hand and stroked it down her cheek. 'That skin you are feeling is only seven years old, Jared. Before that . . . I learnt a great deal about people. I learnt the controls by which I could stop anyone or anything crushing me. I learnt what really mattered to me. You know the most important thing I found out? It's very simple. The least important thing of all, Jared, is skin-deep beauty.'

She took a deep breath, her eyes caressing his with all the love in her heart. 'And now, my darling, you're going to have to learn that too. I wish it weren't so. They are hard, hurtful lessons to learn, and I wouldn't wish them on anyone. But one thing you can count on, Jared...my eyes will never flinch away from you. You will never see me wince, or ask or pray that things could be different. They're not...and that has to be accepted.'

'So that's where your control comes from,' he murmured wonderingly, and Laura plunged on, intent on keeping his mind turning so that the resolution he had come to didn't become fixed.

'Control...and other things, Jared. I made up my own rules to live by. When we met, I sensed the same kind of thing in you.' She smiled, instinctively playing to the reluctant fascination that was creeping into his eyes. 'You called me a savage pagan queen. In my mind, you were a warrior-king who would stride over any world and make it his own. That's something inside you, Jared. Something that strikes a deep response in me. The only man who ever has. And ever will.'

Her voice deepened with her own needs as she continued. 'I know that you love me, Jared. You might never tell me that, and I don't care. Because in my heart of hearts I know you do. Just as I know I love you. To me you are very special...unique...and there is no other man in the world who can take your place. You—the person who lives behind your face—you are *my place*, Jared. That's what is all-important to me. Nothing else. I belong with you. And I will do everything—*everything*—that is humanly possible to keep you with me.'

His hand tightened crushingly around her own. Again she made no protest. This was a time of decision and her whole life-force seemed to be poised, waiting for Jared's answer. Conflicting emotions raged in his eyes for interminable moments, but when at last he spoke, his voice was soft with the relaxed peace of a man who had fought a battle and the outcome was to his liking.

'Mrs Eastern...' there was almost a smile in his words '...you've got yourself a deal. I'm not sure you won't regret it, but you're one hell of a bargainer. And you're one hell of a woman. And this time, you've certainly got yourself a deal.'

Her inner relief poured into a smile that lit her face with a beauty that caught Jared's breath and made him wonder if he had done right to cling to her. But her reply filled him with a sense of rightness that was undeniable.

'Well, Mr Eastern, I did think it was time you were taught a bit of equality. It's all very well saying I'm your partner, but you've got to really mean it. And I aim to keep you to that deal. No matter what.'

'No matter what,' he agreed. And then, after a pause, 'I reckon we'll get along together just fine.'

And although he didn't say the words, the love in his eyes was all that Laura needed. They were together again in mind and heart and spirit, in every way that counted.

As day followed day, there was less and less for Connie Hammond to do. The crisis was passed. Laura saw the restless streak and suggested that Ted would be getting lonely. Her mother was reluctant to go, but was convinced of its good sense. Assured that everything was fine between Laura and her husband, Connie Hammond returned home to Boston, more at peace with herself than she had been in her whole life.

She would bring Ted with her next time she came to Bendeneer Downs—when Laura had her baby. She was sure that Ted would find it a revelation. The lifestyle was just so incredibly different. Not something they would want to live with all the time, of course, but she could now see Laura's point of view. And it would do Ted good to see a different slice of life. Broaden his mind. It was never too late to learn, Connie decided, however hard that might be.

The month that Jared had to remain hospitalised was a severe trial of patience for him, but Laura did all she could to brighten his days. The dressings came off the gashes on his face and she marvelled at what a good job the surgeon had done. Jared glumly declared he looked like the son of Frankenstein's monster, but if that was what turned her on, who was he to complain?

Laura laughed and kissed the self-mocking twist from his lips, kissed the scars that showed his love for her, letting him know that nothing about him could ever be repulsive to her. As each day passed and her attitude never once wavered, Jared relaxed more and more, gradually coming to believe that what he looked like was totally irrelevant to his wife. He even began to dismiss the scars as of no account himself, knowing that one day they would fade, until he was jolted back to the present-day reality by his mother's and Rafe's reaction.

Rafe manfully tried to hide his shock and act naturally, but it was in his eyes and the forced even tenor of his greeting. His mother simply stared at him, tears filling her eyes and running down her cheeks. Jared jerked his head away, his gaze stabbing at Laura who was sitting on the other side of him, holding his hand. Her calm grey eyes bored into his, acknowledging nothing but the person he was inside.

And he knew then...he knew she had been through this...and risen above it. Her inner strength fired the mettle inside him. This was just something he had to live through for a short time, nothing like the years that had been inflicted on Laura. The respect he had for this woman who was his wife swelled to an awe that filled his soul with an exultation he had never known. She was very special...unique...and she belonged to him...and

always would. He squeezed her hand and turned back
to his visitors, determined not to flinch away again.

'My wife assures me that miracles can be performed
by plastic surgeons these days,' he said sardonically. 'So
cheer up, Mother. I'll look a lot better after the next
operation. And if not, what the hell? I've got too much
living to do to worry about a bit of disfigurement.'

Naomi looked wonderingly at Laura, shook her head,
then took a deep breath and faced her son again. 'A lot
of good living. Rafe tells me that what happened was
necessary. It finally puts to rest the ghosts of the past
which——'

'No, Mother,' Jared interrupted firmly. 'The only
ghosts of the past are in people's minds. What happened
was for the future. If that bull had reached Laura, he
could have killed her. All I did was protect my
future...and that of your grandchild.'

'You're very lucky to have Laura as your wife,' his
mother said tentatively, as if she was trying it on for
size, then proceeded more confidently as she looked up
at the man at her side, her expression suggesting that
she was seeing him with new eyes too. 'Just as I'm lucky
to have a husband like Rafe,' she added softly.

An odd look of incredulity passed over Rafe's face.
Then it was as if a glow of hope and happiness beamed
from within and made him look years younger. 'It's good
to be alive,' he said cheerfully, then grinned at Jared.
'How does it feel, now that you know you're going to
be a father?'

From that moment on, the visit proceeded along more
natural lines and even gathered the sense of a family
being together. Naomi startled everyone by saying that
she and Rafe would certainly be visiting Bendeneer
Downs in future to see their grandchild. It was a dec-
laration that the past really was over, and the future was
going to be completely clear of it from now on.

Laura felt a deep pleasure in the thought that it was finally finished with... that the generation of pain was giving way to a new generation... one in which love and family and respect for each other came first... and their child who would be born and nurtured in that atmosphere. What more could anyone want? And nothing would tear that love apart. She wouldn't let it happen. Ever.

Nevertheless, Laura was privately amazed at the way Jared handled himself when he was released from hospital and was faced with normal society again. He didn't seem to mind the covert stares at all. He tossed his head high and walked tall. He was a man, not a child, she reminded herself—a man among men—and her pride in him knew no bounds.

When they returned to Bendeneer Downs, it was he who put everyone at ease with his good-humoured acceptance of his scarred face. Shock and sympathy were quickly erased by everyone's genuine pleasure that he was alive and well and in their midst again. Jared broke open a new case of champagne. Life resumed its normal pace and business as if it had never been interrupted by anything of consequence.

The weeks rolled into months and Laura bemoaned the fact that she was losing her shape. 'I'll have to buy a stack of maternity clothes when we go down to Adelaide for your next operation, Jared,' she declared one morning, failing miserably at trying to zip up her loosest pair of jeans. 'I'm getting positively lumpy.'

He came up behind her, slid his arms around her waist, and caressed the lump in question with tenderly erotic purpose. 'Well, at least you still want me,' she sighed happily, leaning back to savour the warm intimacy between them.

'I'll always want you,' he murmured, teasing her ear with delicate little nibbles.

'Even when I'm all blown up?' she asked anxiously.

He swung her around to face him, but it was not to kiss her. His eyes were not smouldering with desire, but burning with intense emotion. His hand lifted and stroked softly down her cheek.

'No matter what you looked like—or what you ever look like—you're my woman, Laura. The wife of my mind and heart and soul. And no one could ever take your place, because it's so very deeply *your* place. I couldn't untangle myself from you any more, even if I wanted to. And I don't want to. I know you don't need me to say these things, but sometimes I need to say them, Laura.'

And the need swirled around her, engulfed her, merging her with him more intimately than any physical act could ever do.

'I want you to know that I felt it too—the something in you which called to me,' Jared continued, the intensity of the moment glittering in his eyes. 'It was why I married you. Why I couldn't hold myself apart from you even though my own self-preservation dictated it. You answer everything I've ever wanted. To say—I love you—it's too simple, Laura. I'll love our child. But you...'

He wrapped his arms around her and crushed her to him. 'You I hold on to. You I'll never let go,' he whispered through the soft tresses of her hair.

And she felt his heart beating against hers, with hers...and knew that all the doors were open at last. They would never shut again.

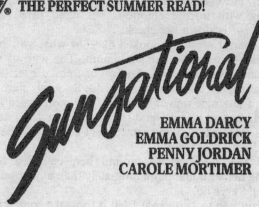

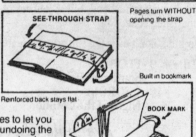

Back by Popular Demand

Janet Dailey
Americana

A romantic tour of America through fifty favorite Harlequin Presents® novels, each set in a different state researched by Janet and her husband, Bill. A journey of a lifetime in one cherished collection.

In June, don't miss the sultry states featured in:

Title # 9 - **FLORIDA**
         Southern Nights
  #10 - **GEORGIA**
         Night of the Cotillion

Available wherever Harlequin books are sold.